Published by Apocalypse Party
Book Design by Mike Corrao
Cover Design by Vich
Erohazard Divider Icon by Evan

Paperback: 978-1-954899-71-1

TORTURE WORKS

Porpentine

CONTENTS

Subhuman

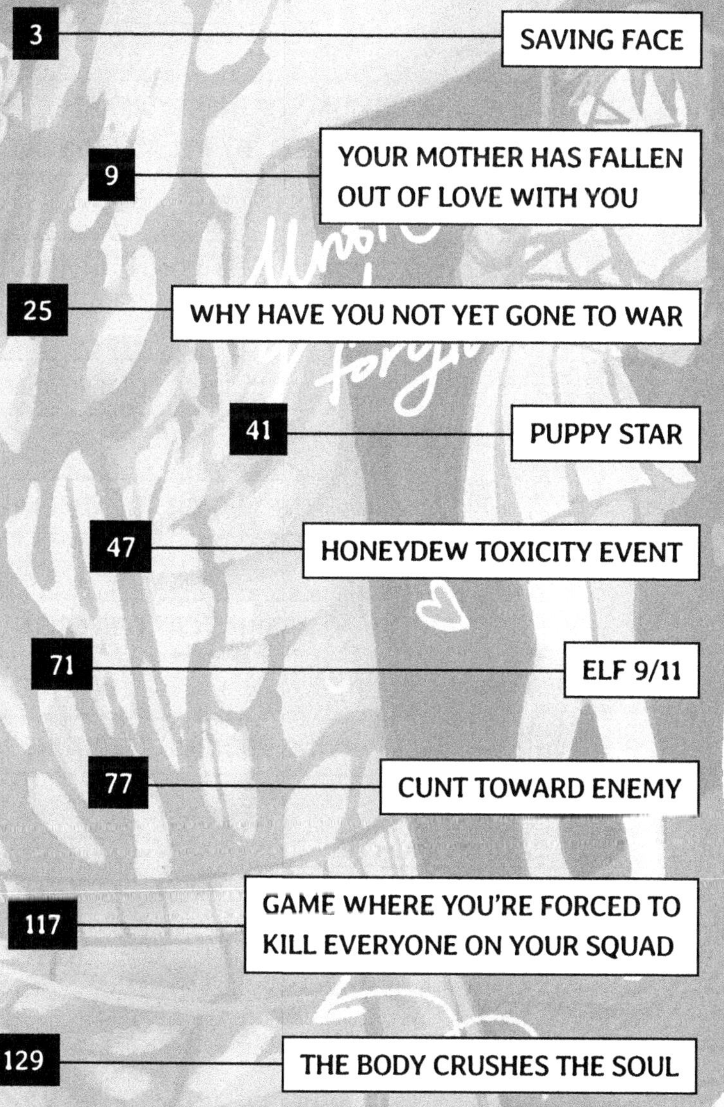
XRAFSTAR!!

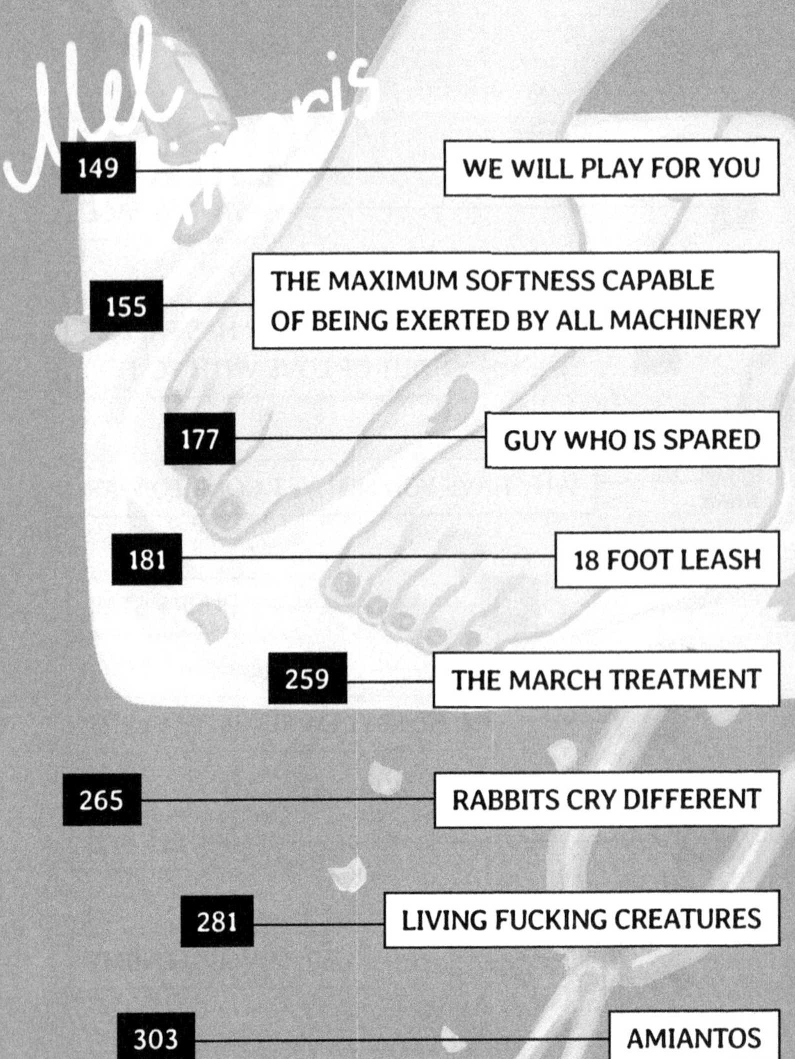

SAVING FACE

The boss's son always tells me to bite their ears off, I don't wanna bite their ears off, I have texture issues with the cartilage. But in the end, I'd bite all night for him. They don't even look human when I'm done. Then again, neither do I.

You gotta leave some face though. Or you don't have a reference point.

I spin the chair around. It's so light without the guy on it. Just a red shadow on the seat.

"Anything else I can do for you?"

The boss's son says, "You've got something in your teeth."

I pick it out with the nail I keep sharp for this purpose. I don't even know what that was. I get deep in there, you know. Scientists discover new body parts every day. I love that. It keeps me hopeful.

"I was saying, anything else I can do for you?"

But he's already back in the swimming pool, deaf with water. I watch his limbs ripple like what I'm digesting in my stomach.

After watching me work, the boss's son won't let me suck his dick anymore.

I guess once you become the dog, you're useful in a different way. He won't soil himself with beasts. Or he simply doesn't want to get his dick bit off.

But I don't think my teeth are sharper than any other guy. It's strictly mental.

The doctor says I have a tapeworm. Could explain a few things. He wants to give me some Praziquantel. The label says EXPELS TAPERED AHRIMANFORMS. I tell him I'm not shitting out my honor and my value and my devotion. Not unless God himself sucks it out of me.

He says, take the vermifuge. You never know.

Leave enough face for the funeral, Carafe says. He's old school. Thinking of his family.

I look to the boss's son for approval. He's filing his nails and I wish they were my teeth. He says, sure.

I say, no promises, but I'll start from the toes, and we'll see how it goes.

Carafe says, oky doky.

I hop up and down, trying to make the cigarette smoke hit my lungs faster.

The boss's son says, "What are you doing?"

"Nothing. I'm good to go."

"Let me see your teeth."

I open my mouth wide like the dentist. He looks inside, eyes narrowed. I'm open so long I start drooling, then I start sweating

He finally says, "Is your stomach empty?"

"I could make it be empty."

"I just want to make sure this goes smoothly. We're doing two guys tonight."

"Two. Wow."

"Is that a problem?"

"Maybe for them, if you know what I mean, hehe-heh."

He takes the cigarette from my fingers and sniffs it. He's quitting, but it's hard. I know the longer he smells it, the harder it'll get. I watch to see what he'll do.

Two chairs, two guys, one of them is actually a lady, but you can't tell anymore. I believe in equality of the sexes. But it's hard biting through some of these guys. The piercings, tattoos, gelled hair. Eating a woman is like eating two or three kids stacked on top of each other. Walk in the park. And to be frank, I needed the assist. Never did two guys at the same time before. Wasn't sure I could. But I'd never say no to the boss's son. I'll keep singing even if my voice breaks, as long as the camera stays on me.

YOUR MOTHER HAS FALLEN OUT OF LOVE WITH YOU

Rain sweeps cold and black from the sea, palm fronds slithering across the hotel parking lot. It's the holidays and people sing in a church across the street.

The man is slim and dark-haired and wears a suit under a transparent rain jacket. The boy wears a black poncho covering most of his body, black wet hair plastered over his face so it looks like a ragged fringe of the hood.

"A room for me and my son." He wraps his arm around the boy with a warm smile, clear insulation over glistening black.

The hydrophobic jacket drops to the floor, carpet darkening around the clear plastic. The man stretches, knuckles popping. His suitcase falls over, heavy and swollen. The boy's suitcase is hollow-cheeked and empty.

The man flops on the bed and the boy remains standing, holding a roll of leather under his arm like a small rug. The man turns on the television. Weather advisory. Shopping channel. Pay-per-view. Insect documentary. Censored videolaga, red mosaics vibrating as a wizard's knife glides through a palace.

He looks at the boy.

Why are you wearing clothes in here?

The boy hesitates, then lifts his poncho, black plastic stretching taut over his face. It crinkles as he drags it from his body like a garbage bag.

He takes his shirt off. His skin is covered in bruises.

He removes his pants. His knees are pocked with scars.

He pulls down his underwear.

He shivers in the cold.

The man mutes the television. He cocks his head as if listening for something. His hand perches on the remote control like a pale mantis on a black branch.

The boy places the leather object on the floor and rolls it open. The interior is covered in spikes.

The man leans on the bed and rests his head in his hand, watching the boy like he was watching the television.

The boy sinks his knees onto the leather strip with a sharp gasp, spikes digging into the thin skin stretched over his patellas.

The man picks up the phone.

Hello, room service?

He twists the kinky cord around his finger, sock foot bobbing to an unheard beat.

Can I get a coffee? Cat-eye. Yessir. And it says here you have the finest chocolate chip fudge pie. I'll have a big slice of that. Mmhm. Mmhm.

He looks at the boy.

And can I get some macaroni and cheese. Thank you. Thank you so much.

On the TV screen, a hamburger rotates, dripping with juice, special sauce spilling over, raining pink into the abyss. Bright lights explode behind it.

The boy's stomach growls.

Wave after wave of pain and numbness radiate from his knees. He knows each wave as it burns through him. His joints are inflamed, spikes cooking the viscous raw egg of his synovial fluid.

The food arrives.

The man eats with great pleasure, sucking the underside of his spoon.When the macaroni and cheese is cold, he places the bowl on the floor.

Are you hungry?

Spread your legs. Like a frog.

The man wraps a napkin around his fingers.

The boy's thighs tremble from staying open, toes curling as the man mashes the macaroni inside. It breaks apart and he gathers it up again and pushes until the inside is full of the paste and chunk of it.

The boy puts his hand on his stomach, afraid of losing control, the boundary between his body and the food distorted. He shouldn't have done that. He puts his hand on the carpet. He knows it's too late.

The man stands up and slides the dirty napkin from his fingers. They are long and slender and pristine.

The boy quivers on the floor, rubbing his legs together.

You can eat that when it comes out.

The boy's fingers dig into the carpet. Dark hair quivers and shakes, blinding him. His tongue scrapes the inside of his mouth, trying to lick the taste away. He can't open his mouth because it would make the floor dirty. Saliva builds, thick and chunky until he forces himself to swallow. It replaces itself with bile, and the bad taste remains.

The man sits on the bed and stares at him.

Am I beautiful?

Am I beautiful?

Am I beautiful?

Am I beautiful?

Am I beautiful?

Am I beautiful?

Am I beautiful?

Am I beautiful?

Am I beautiful?

Yes, the boy says. When he speaks, he can taste his digestive tract.

The man reclines on the bed with an arched leg and a demure smile.

Well, if you insist.

The man checks the windows. Night, buzzing night, old wiring and neon like dying nerves. The room is full of cleaning chemicals, he senses them like pepper spray lingering on the air.

He enters the bathroom and closes the door.

Something squeals like a pig, long and tortured.

His eyes are so bright, people barely notice anything else. But he is only himself when the lights are off. His silhouette seems like the purest version of him.

He watches the boy for a long time. The boy can only move in small ways.

The man speaks.

Your mother has fallen out of love with you.

The man puts a tape in a cassette player. He puts on headphones so the boy can't hear. The man only listens to muzak.

Confess your happy thoughts to me.

You know I can read your mind.

The boy confesses.

Earlier I looked out the car window.

The man smiles.

You're not allowed to look up.

I know. I'm sorry.

The man says, gently: what did you see?

The boy starts crying.

The man smiles. They sit in silence.

The man hurts him badly.

After kneeling on the spike strip for an hour, the boy finally speaks.

Do you love me?

The man bursts out laughing.

The man strips film from a cassette tape. The magnetic ribbon wafts into a wastebasket. He places the empty tape back in his player.

The headphones are clamped on the boy's ears.

Click.

Can you hear?

Do you see?

(The clink of cutlery on a plate.)

(Silence.)

(The bed creaks.)

I'll always find you.

In the womb.

(Or was it, the room? It's hard to hear through the hot towel, so tight it feels like his brain will burst.)

If you found me, you could save yourself.

The radiator hates him with an infinite suffocating heat. It chars the air that enters his mouth. It plugs his nostrils with two hot slugs.

Turn around.

It burns what little soft flesh is behind him. He tightens his shoulder blades and cheeks against the red-hot knives of air.

Relax.

The man's voice enters his spine. His shoulders slump. A tear of sweat slips down his flushed back, the flat surface exposed evenly to the heat. Lower down, the radiator breathes into his smallest place, sanding it with teeth of newborn glass.

An ugly vacuum of despair in his throat.

The man leaves the room.

When he comes back, he inspects the imprints on the carpet. The boy hasn't moved. His skin is peeling like a lizard.

You have two choices.

You can endure this for an hour.

Or you can move four inches back. And burn yourself.

Would you rather have an hour, or a permanent scar?

The man holds out a flower, small and pink, picked from a narrow strip of grass outside. The boy looks away, trembling.

The flower glides closer and the boy turns the opposite direction.

The man moves faster, whipping the flower to the left and right. The boy desperately tries to avoid looking at it.

The flower is in his face. He jerks back, falling over because his hands are tied.

The man smiles. He takes a fork from his plate, the metal encrusted with red sauce. He holds it out, handle first.

The boy stares at it, breathing heavily.

In three seconds, I will flip it around.

The boy scrambles to get back on his knees. He pushes at the carpet with his bunched hands, wiggling his bound legs up and down as he backs onto the fork. He cries out at the cold touch of stainless steel, the unlubricated metal burning the deeper inside it goes.

The man unplugs the lamp. The room is dark. Rain grinds against the window.

The man makes a V-sign with his fingers, pale enough to be visible in the low light. They frame the wall socket, three black holes.

Put it inside.

The boy crawls backwards, clenching to keep the fork from falling out. His toes touch the wall and he stops. His emaciated ribs swell like claws, jerking with quick tight breaths.

Five seconds.

The fork taps the plastic of the socket, tap tap tap, scuttle, tap.

Don't scream.

The boy's mouth stretches so wide his face seems to disappear, like a piece of white paper burnt black from beneath.

His skinny muscles contort, every part of him suddenly catching the shadows in dimpling pools of contortion.

The carpet darkens under him.

Smoke hisses from between his legs.

That was six seconds.

The man reaches for his plate.

The rhythmic crash of cars through puddles. Shadows flit across the curtains. A boy laughs, skipping quickly with his parents to their room.

More laughter and giggling. Brisk chatter. The doors of the church open and music comes out. The doors slam shut.

You've been doing the things I said.

Are you ready for your one hug?

The boy's mouth opens. He does that to keep his face from making the shape he is not allowed to make.

He opens his suitcase.

It is empty.

It is full of spikes. They line the interior.

The boy crawls inside. Each movement requires a deep intake of breath, as he forces his limbs as tight as possible. He lays there, legs crushed so tight against his chest that his stomach hurts, the smell between his legs funneled up between his knees. His hands are folded back over his shoulders, digging into the fibers of his trapezius.

The suitcase shuts.

Darkness.

He can't move a centimeter in any direction. He is sinking onto spikes or jammed against spikes at every angle. The vibration of his heart and lungs is enough to sting him all over.

Silence.

The man's fingers brush the exterior.

Click. Click. Latches locked.

Silence.

Copper tendrils of scent ooze from the walls. Blood like stars.

Silence.

Stomach growling.

The smell of leather mixes with his unwashed body, harsh and rotten and chemical.

Darkness.

Darkness.

Blinding images explode from the black. He shuts his eyes but they're already shut. He turns his head and spikes stab his lips, jam into his nose, prick phosphenes through his eyelids. He forces himself to remain still.

Wetness drips through his hair and from his eyes and it's all the same color in the dark.

The curtains begin to glow.

Sun spills across the carpet.

The man wraps his arms around the suitcase. He rests his head on it, smiling, and squeezes tight.

WHY HAVE YOU NOT YET GONE TO WAR

On that day, I was supposed to go to the festival and trade my knife in. I was supposed to meet the old man at his table and hand it over. This was a promise I made to him, after a long and serious discussion. He was the kind of dignified old man who did not become angry, only disappointed. The kind where silence became its own condemnation, not from him, necessarily, but because you were reminded of every good thing you were letting down. Something fine and noble in the universe reflected off him, bouncing from some unknown source beyond my own access. So the promise had some weight to me.

The festival was to be held at the high school, on the lawn and parking lot, with all kinds of tables and booths. There was even supposed to be an animal of some kind there, for entertainment.

But first, I went for a hike with friends, out on the coast where the land split off almost like an island, but still attached, a jumble of water, trees, stone, and brush, spilling through each other around a high rocky formation, almost like a butte, but eroded and overgrown.

They weren't my friends. I liked them fine, but we were really just acquaintances, held together by a few common links here and there. If we had known each other better, maybe things wouldn't have gone the way they did.

We shared a small device, a kind of portable heater. It burnt into vapor a small amount of plant matter that had been prepared for that purpose, a common and recreational plant byproduct which had cognitive effects considered by some to be entertaining, warm, and easy. I inhaled some myself, and we proceeded in a meandering way along the side of the rock mass. The path began to shrink.

J__ pointed ahead and to the right. I saw it too. The path was above a sheer cliff, which we had somehow not noticed due to our mild intoxication. The ocean was far below.

Nope, I thought to myself. Nope to that broken and barely there path. This is how people die in stupid circumstances.

Then someone said something, and I saw it again. It was a trick of refraction, and most of all, our own drugged distortion. The water was shallow and clear and the same level as the path. We had not risen in altitude at all and were safely at sea level. It was a broken path, with water running through the cracks of it, but the sea it came from was shallows, which you could see to the bottom of.

We continued along the path, slowly, smiling, abashed but in good humor, and it was then that it happened. Something whooshed by me at incredible speed, like a bird darting low over the water to spear a fish. I looked around and saw nothing. Then another knife shot past my head.

"Is someone throwing knives?" B__ said.

M__ laughed incredulously.

Run, I said.

But even as we ran, I had a doomed feeling. We had no time for strategy, and especially for coordination. We did not share a fundamental understanding with each other, a bond of time and trust that would have allowed instinctual cooperation. We were being funneled into the rocky tunnels, away from land and emergency services, into true isolation.

We ran up a crude tunnel of stairs carved into the rock, becoming breathless from the exertion. At least we were going up instead of down, toward light instead of dark, I imagine was everyone's feeling. As we reached the end, M__ went first, hauling herself up through the hole where the stairs ended. A knife hit her in the face, and she reeled. I thought she would fall back toward us, but she had some footing, had lifted herself at the exact moment she was struck, and she fell on the ground above and was dragged away, shoes disappearing from the sky.

We stood there, caught between that sky and the sound of pursuers coming up behind us.

They took us to the top of the rock mass, which was covered in grass and even a few trees. There was a store there, a medium-sized supermarket. It was slightly clean inside and the shelves were stocked.

Our captors did not speak to us. We sat on various surfaces, waiting for their unknown deliberations to conclude. They were dressed in minimal, utilitarian, outdoor clothing of reasonable quality.

I wondered if M__ was dead. We had not seen her body. Her absence was as effective as their refusal to speak.

R__ pointed at me. "Don't you have a knife?"

"Does this knife gang have anything to do with you?" B__ said.

"Why didn't you use your knife?"

I could have explained to them how the knife wouldn't do anything in outnumbered circumstances, against many knives thrown from hiding. I could have had a good story for myself as well: I chose not to use my knife. I chose the way of peace.

But the truth is, I forgot I had it. As if part of me had already gone to the festival, and handed it in, and kept my promise. But I had not kept my promise, and I had not been truly tested.

I listened to the people around me, theorizing and arguing about this situation beyond their understanding. They were precisely the kind of nothing people one meets on a day like today, a day between lives. I was nothing, so they were nothing too. I would only know I had begun to live a different life when I stopped meeting such nothing people and met a being of totality. Until then, I would get what I deserved.

I looked at my captors until one of them caught my eyes. "I have an appointment at the festival."

He said nothing.

"If I'm not there, they'll notice."

Two of them escorted me to the high school. Close-cropped hair, one blond, the other dark, wearing jeans and jackets. Their knives were close and hidden.

A bright day, the high school lawn green and white, covered in tables and booths.

We passed the gorilla enclosure. We did not slow down, so I only perceived it from the corner of my eye as a presence of power. One of nature's animals. Even in my periphery, it had a subtly deforming quality, as if the humans around it were judged by contrast. It felt similar to the mechanism of the old man's presence, yet in the service of an entirely opposite force. If the old man caused one to consider the path of peace, the gorilla asked you why you had not yet gone to war. I do not say that because I believe every primate to be inherently vicious, but because this was what they called a fool-thrasher gorilla, a gorilla that thrashes fools. Anyone could see it by the markings and pelt, if they had even a little curiosity about the ways a gorilla can manifest and become. It would be absurd to think a gorilla had the same ideas about fools as we do, or even knew they existed. I merely mean that whatever instincts are useful to such a gorilla in the wilderness, within its particular hierarchy and the biological imperative of it all, mapped perfectly upon the human concept of a fool.

To many, it would appear an ordinary gorilla, and this is a lie I would not have minded telling myself, three hundred sixty-four days of the year. But this was not one of those days. On such a day, even a small lie felt permanent.

We continued up the steps of the high school lawn, passing a hammer show. Many people are amused by a hammer of unordinary size. The hammer man swung his hammer back and forth, and the crowd clapped and cheered. I would not have been surprised if at some point, more wrinkles were added to the dynamic, and the hammer was employed in some sort of false game or athletic trick. But it was like the gorilla, something felt in my periphery, the heavy object reduced to the flutter of a paper fan.

In this bright part of town, in this bright part of day, away from the yellow air and pollen murk of the coast, one could imagine the knife gang and the supermarket and all that was a fantasy of some kind. But the intoxicant had worn off and I felt only a cold, captive clarity, chained to each moment. I was there to perform my previous plans as hollow ritual, to reenact what I had not yet done.

The old man was at the top of the steps. He sat at a simple table like you might see at any church potluck or a meeting for people with problems, the kind where faux-wood texture is applied with adhesive. He was perfectly still. It seemed, perhaps, enough at his age to absorb the most simple facts of the world. To take the sun on his face, the gentle wind through his long white hair, these things that are left after one's earlier years have been spent chasing heat and strife and desire. If the men with knives had vanished at that moment, I believe I could have joined him with equal equanimity.

But the men remained, with their denim jackets and their knives, peripheral as a gorilla and a hammer.

The old man's eyes shifted, nearly imperceptibly. Or perhaps it was his lips, or head, or nostrils. Perhaps nothing had moved at all. I placed my knife, small and bronze, at the corner of the table, as far from him as I could without it falling to the ground.

"It won't contaminate me."

"I know," I said, in the nearly cheating but perhaps understandable way of someone who has only come to know at the second they speak.

We stayed in silence. His skin was deeply gnarled and cracked like wood. Mazes of wisdom in which one could easily fall into a meditative state. But I felt the knife gang at my back, insensitive to the power of the moment. But at least they were quiet, for their own closed, limited reasons. They were content to wait for me to complete the ritual, to leave no suspicion when I disappeared. These were clean, neat, and professional men, who many might go their whole lives without meeting. But I had become caught in the narrow mechanism of their purpose.

The moment ran out.

I said, "Thank you." As the words emerged, they were bent by pain and fragility and longing. I desired, with the strain of heartbreak, to tell him what was happening. But I could not beg for help. I could not even alarm him, or he would be endangered by his own good qualities, and worst of all (such was my selfish thinking at that time), become witness to the ugliness which was attached to me. And it would happen in the sight of my knife.

So I let this pain pass between us, into his great receptivity and silence and dignity, hoping only, perhaps, to be witnessed in some small way, without fanfare, without excruciation.

Behind me, I could hear the limits of their silence, and perhaps others waiting to see the old man for their own reasons, at this table placed here for this purpose. So I stepped away before the perfect silence could be damaged.

As we walked down the steps, we passed the gorilla enclosure. I paused to stare at it, knowing they would accept this brief reprieve. The sight of a gorilla is a kind of truce, even among the most divided hearts.

The gorilla's hands were wrapped around the bars of the enclosure. It rocked against them, as if soothing itself. The movements were so small I thought nothing of them. Gradually, I came to think it was a form of exercise, and that the movements really were more energetic than I thought. The way the bars rotated and bent by centimeters was calming to look at.

We continued down the steps. The hammer show was still ongoing, but it was only a man with a hammer, and I knew I could not stop for such a thing. Anyone may become a man with a hammer.

We passed between tables of snacks, and I wondered if the knife men would stop for those. All men, fundamentally, at some point in their lives, will eat food. But this was not such a moment. They ignored the foil covered in flattened frosting, and the individual pieces of corn floating inside ice cubes.

After a few more steps, we became aware of a commotion behind us.

We looked back and saw the gorilla holding the hammer. Some laughed, while others made tutting sounds. But no one spoke, until one person finally said, "Is there no handler for that gorilla?" It was the hammer man, who you can imagine having an investment in the proceedings. The hammer was large and non-standard, red-handled with a black head. It almost seemed to be a plastic mallet, but the heaviness of it would have been palpable even to someone who couldn't win a jellybean contest with an empty jar.

The gorilla swung the hammer with such a long and loose reach that I thought it would sail from the tips of his fingers and fly away. He swung to either side, clearing the tables and booths from the lawn as he descended the steps. The men ran toward their car, but he ambled in front of them. Perhaps he did not single them out for who they were, but because they moved so quickly. Which is perhaps the same thing.

The gorilla screamed and pounded the ground with the hammer, breaking the sidewalk into chips, quickening the erosion of years into a single second.

The men screamed and fell on the ground and raised their hands.

The gorilla screamed back, swinging the hammer and banging fat gouges of earth from the lawn. The men screamed and trembled on the ground. The gorilla smashed the sidewalk into many pieces, revealing whatever lies beneath sidewalks. The men shuddered at this loud sound and made many noises. The gorilla banged steadily on the ground like a huge child with a huge toy. The men shuddered from the vibrations. The gorilla screamed at them. The first man screamed, then the second man. The gorilla lifted the hammer high and crashed it down again, knocking up sidewalk far from where it was standing. The men cried out, unintelligible and weeping. The gorilla screamed and its mouth opened so far it seemed to eclipse its head. You don't think of a gorilla as being like a snake, but this is what the mouth looked like, stretched so tall and so sharp. You could not look away, the screaming at a constant pitch which suspended all thought, paralyzed every muscle. Ugly, ugly, ugly, red and black, a tunnel absorbing all light.

The gorilla waddled over to the car we came in and bashed it with such force that the front and back of the car folded together and touched. The men tried to rise to their feet. The gorilla came back and screamed at them. They bowed their heads and became still, but also screaming.

I looked up the steps. A single table remained, with the old man still sitting in exactly the same spot. Everything below him was destroyed.

The gorilla hunched on the grass, breathing heavily, his burly form seeming to slide against itself like dark brown boulders.

The men could not scream anymore. Their breathing was muffled by the dirt.

The old man walked down the steps so quietly that I did not realize until he passed me. He held my knife in his hands, the bronze old and tainted against the simple fresh colors of day.

He came up to the gorilla and placed the knife on the ground. The gorilla picked it up and swallowed it. There was no sound.

The men lay on the ground, starting sometimes as if to get up or crawl away, but they never completed any of these movements. They were like the grass around them, trembling in the breeze.

The old man walked in one direction and the gorilla in another. I stood between them, feeling the diminishment of their polarities. I looked at the sidewalk with its many cracks. I looked down at my hands, which were made open and clear by the sun.

After some time, I walked too, and the direction did not matter.

PUPPY STAR

I get in a fight in the lobby. But the manager calls the director, and the director is in the auditorium watching the premiere with everyone else, and he says, "They're going wild for him in here."

So I don't get thrown out. I head back to the auditorium, but I don't go in. I don't want to see my big mug all over the screen. That puppy dog face makes me sick, except when I don't see myself, which makes me sick. I'm not the main star. But I'm pretty big in it. Kind of. Some nonsense with a gun, and that business with my brother, el star primo. He's only my brother in the movie. In real life, he couldn't give a damn. Where's the esprit de corp.

I hang around the Walmart section of the movie theater. It doesn't feel like Walmart. Just a few slanted rows displaying Hallmark cards and so forth, on the garish zig-zagging carpet.

The director comes out. Intermission.

"Sonny," he says, warmly enough that I decide to take a chance.

"I've been thinking a lot about my role. Trying to go deep."

"That a fact."

"I'm intense. Intense and disgusting. A disgusting little man in a room. Greasy. Boozing. Women. Night. Night piss. I can't see. I see too much. Boneless females on my shit. So intense. So shrill. Choking on whiskey. All over my clothes. So intense. Can't hold my gun. Hand like a claw. Trying to bite my gun into the right shape. So intense—"

He slaps me. No part of him acknowledges what just happened, he only stares old and lumpy at nothing. Then suddenly, he launches into his own hardboiled pastiche. "It was a dirty town. Whiskey and cigarettes. I never should have gotten involved with those. Dames."

"Very good, sir."

He points at the stationery and gift section for our previous presidente. Presidentay.

Solemnly, as if imparting great wisdom, he says, "Don't forget about this guy."

"No sir."

I look at the merchandise. Wehrmacht-themed stationery and gift boxes. It's so funny that he doesn't know I myself am of an ethnoreligious people quite ironic to this conversation. I say something smarmy like, "I love what he did for the REDACTED RACES."

The director nods seriously. I regret everything. The audience won't stop clapping.

HONEYDEW TOXICITY EVENT

>mom comes in
>anon why are there one million mountain dew bottles
>mountain dew is a complete protein dont be a faggot mom
>dumb cunt looks at me like i just blew her fucking mind
Do you fuck your mom?
she's a faggot and you're a butt baby
AIDS baby
hydrofags ITT
water made my sister bipolar
Mountain Drew
Rapyed
Anon has a serious problem and we need to be sensitive. If you don't get your hydration purely from pussy juice kys

call it au jus the way you're penciling roasties
only walls homies getting are when he activates onetap

I wake up in the morning and just lay there looking at the Mountain Dew bottles sparkle in the sliver of sun that gets through my blinds, liquid green plastic glittering. I don't get fat so I can eat all the sugar I want. One time my friend dared me and I drank a bottle of maple syrup. Bubbles of nasty liquid stuck to my keyboard like sap, but I frag around it. When I was a kid, I got into Dew with the limited-edition Game Fuel (Mango Heat) flavor, the promo for Titanfall 2, good ass game until hackers raped it to death RIP.

I post my pic one time as a joke, and someone says I look like doomer boy/e-boy wojak and asks why I have so much Mountain Dew and I say why does your dad fuck you at night. My hair is getting in my face though which damages my gaming potential. But even with my headphones tight, I'm not top fragging anymore, so I'm like haha I'm on vacation, playing on touchpad. But it just gets worse, misclick, DPS diff, my friend Justin makes a joke like wow Overwatch has a really diverse playerbase, they even let blind people play. I say I'm still on vacation, sorry wageslaves :sunglasses: and I switch to support. My mom asks me what I'm playing because she doesn't respect my privacy and streamsnipes my fucking life, and I'll be healing Justin so we can push obj and I'll be like uh yeah that's a cancer beam and I'm killing his ass.

I kept feeling weird but at my e-visit with my doctor I didn't know how to explain I'm suddenly bad at video games, like she already gives me Adderall so there's not much else she can do.

A few days later, I wake up and there's gross shit in my mouth and I spit it out. It looks like vegetables but I don't eat those. I look closer and there's leaves and petals in there. I look it up and it sounds kind of like pica but that's a bitch disease for preggers. There's a more masculine version like Nebuchadnezzar II ate grass and thought he was an oxen and he was chad. Anyways, if you don't remember doing something, it basically didn't happen.

Fucked up dreams. It's like ants ants ants constantly touching me with antennae but it's deep dream ants so they look like yugioh cards and weeb shit and sometimes real people. I'm greentexting my problem like haha wouldn't that be crazy, but no one has any advice for my fake problem that's actually real.

You're either jerking off too much or not enough. What's your coordinate on the Austerlin gradient?

has anon considered not drinking so much sody pop?

I can think of another Sweet Dew Incident that also involved a guy without balls.

watch out for ants bro lmao

>"We believe that ants could use the tranquillising chemicals in their footprints to maintain a populous 'farm' of aphids close to their colony, to provide

honeydew on tap. Ants have even been known to occasionally eat some of the aphids themselves, so subduing them in this way is obviously a great way to keep renewable honeydew and prey easily available."

>The ants have been known to bite the wings off the aphids in order to stop them from getting away and depriving the ants of one of their staple foods: the sugar-rich sticky honeydew which is excreted by aphids when they eat plants. Chemicals produced in the glands of ants can also sabotage the growth of aphid wings.

stunted aphidcels be dewposting

Maybe all this greentext is fucking up my brain. I need to get out of the house. I get my hoodie on and go past my mom, passed out like usual, and what do I see when I go outside? More green shit. It's like people can't get enough fucking grass or something. And big trees, totally unkempt, bark crumbling and sap oozing out, cathedral shit, you ever see how ugly a tree is? It's like gargoyle skin cracked armor flaky pancakes just sloughing off, holes and knots and tree tumors, you see it everywhere. I don't know why people have so many fucking trees in their fucking lawns or spilling out the back of their yards, you even go to the strip mall and there's a tree all chained up with a collar tight around its neck. I can't breathe in this hoodie. I pull it off and I'm going to get a sunburn but fuck if I'm getting shade from something with that many leaves, so thick and close together, sun pushing you up close to the big knots of sap all glistening and gooey, you can't trust it.

I get dizzy and maybe blackout or something. I see Miku and her big fat green hair waving around and normally I'd be down but the way it moves is very upsetting to me, like big hairy antennae, and she's probing my face and I'm like stop it and her huge bug eyes just stare at me and I'm spitting at her trying to get the hair out and I wake up on the grass and a cat is licking me. I get to a park restroom and wash my face off to prevent toxoplasmosis, a bipolar female disease I definitely don't need, and the water touches my lips and I think, maybe I should be drinking water and not just Mountain Dew all the time. So I bend over like a water fountain but it tastes like shit and I spit it out. I picked a bad day to start drinking water. And they probably put the nastiest, most disgusting water in park restrooms specifically. I go home and crack open one of my mom's Smart-Waters and that tastes awful too, so I dump it out.

I go back to my room and can finally breathe again. Going outside was a fucking mistake. I put on the Saints Row: The Third soundtrack and try to make my brain shut the fuck up. I pop an addy and autoplay a bunch of stuff on Youtube and a 2000s commercials compilation comes up and I remember the ones I loved as a kid like the World of Warcraft Mountain Dew ad where two milfs are in a supermarket and one pulls a SWORD FROM HER CART and the other turns into a BIG MUSCLY ORC and the other one turns into the PURPLE ELF who is PURPLE LIKE WIDOWMAKER ALSO BY BLIZZARD WHAT THE FUCK and they're basically naked in the supermarket and fucking it up but my favorite was the Mountain Dew Transformation Commercial (2005), so fucking hilarious I love the effect they have for the car changing, exploding all over the place and snapping back again, I could watch it explode for hours. Then the guy points the car remote at his friend and the other guy grows long hair and tits, then his jeans roll up super tight into a cutoff denim skirt and his head SPASMS like some Jacobs Ladder shit (the inspiration for Silent Hill btw dope game) and he's a girl and her generic shitty drink snaps into a Dew and she's like how about a Dew and I'm chugging as I watch it, green and sweet and sugary and green and—

I'm so sweaty and so hot I actually go to take a shower but I get this bad feeling as the water is shooting up the pipes and I'm standing there naked and I put up my hands but it's too late, the water hits me and I'm in fucking shock, I'm tripping over shit and I land on the floor and I'm just shuddering with mammalian gag reflex or whatever, trying to wipe the water off me with a towel. I keep wiping, but for some reason I can't get it all, and that's when I see green on the towel, I'm dripping, I think I've got Dew ass, one of those crazy things you read about from drinking too much Mountain Dew. I need to put something else in my body, so I order Papa Johns but I'm only able to drink three of the extra garlic sauce cups. I just can't get into the pizza, especially after I eat all the pineapple toppings and it's just greasy cheese left. I ask my mom if she wants my leftover pizza and she says why would I want your leftover pizza that you ate the toppings off like a bird. I say I don't know mom and go back to my room.

The next week is hard, really hard, I'm sleeping all the time and burning all over and I get so fucking dirty and sweaty. I wait for my mom to go to Hobby Lobby and I go into the shower but I don't turn the water on, I have a gallon of Mountain Dew and I unscrew it, almost dropping the whole thing, feel so shaky with all this sugar in my system, I don't think I've eaten much this week except Apple Jacks with Dew instead of milk, but I even switched to healthy cereal (Kix) but my heart is still pounding all the time. I manage to lift the jug and pour it on me and it gets in my hair and I get that mammalian gag reflex again like AHHHH HHH AHHHHH HHHHH and I can't see and it's sticky all over my body getting in my pubic hair and between my toes and I have to sit down and it's wet on my ass but I'm finally able to get clean and I keep scrubbing with my mom's loofah and listening to soda gurgle down the drain and each time I squeeze the loofah out, I lick the sticky drippings.

I get out and turn on the shower to rinse it out so my mom won't yell at me, then I go to sleep and if I have dreams I don't remember them. I think I'm finally getting a grip. I haven't used my computer for at least twenty minutes. I'm Kaczynski out here. I'm zen. I'm enlightened. I'm top lane with perfect CS. I have a tarp on my floor that I sleep on so my blankets don't stick to my skin and get it all linty. It crinkles a lot when I move so I don't move, except to eat more cereal out of the bag and some of my mom's Luna bars, which actually taste pretty fucking good, and drink my Dew and fall asleep again. I think I have that paradoxical ADHD thing where caffeine and sugar is actually good for you and help you fall asleep and be normal.

Blacking out a lot. I think it's a special kind of supersleep that probably is more nutritional and healthy for you. I feel like a perfect machine, like an alien bug that can just power off and on like a computer. I stockpiled enough Dew to stay in my bedroom for a while. It's the perfect system because I piss exactly as much as I drink into the bottles, which become empty because I drank them. It's perfect cosmic fucking Egyptian balance, fucking Greek philosopher shit. I know what you're thinking but this is a cool experiment and it'll be a lot of laughs and everything will be normal soon. I have an ironic perspective and I'm capable of seeing the situation realistically so I'm going to just ride this out until I have enough energy and can find some water that isn't fucked like the water in our pipes. But my mom keeps delaying the process by banging on the door and fucking up my concentration, talking about her plants being missing and I need to set out poison for the rabbits or whatever. The sugar is itching all over and flies are everywhere so I decide (free will) to man up and deal with this shit, so I watch some Peterson until my brain feels normal and I take a couple Addys and go to the backyard and spray myself down and the water, as expected, looks, tastes, smells like shit but I do it super fast and I'm freaking out and I forgot a towel so I wipe it off with my shirt, walking around going HOOWA HOOWA and my mom's plants look garbage, all torn up and the orange tree is wrinkled, ridged, makes you want to run your hair hand across it, all the cracks and peeling, I kick it, so angry for some reason, and tear off as much bark as I can. Rotten oranges squish under my toes, flies jump from the moldy peel onto my feet and I kick them off but they keep nipping on my ankles. My ADHD is driving me fucking insane.

I go back inside and my skin is irritated from having high fructose corn syrup on it for so long, which doctors never talk about for some reason but at least I'm clean now. This'll be a crazy story to tell people. The worst is when you don't have anything to post, just sit there thinking of something to say so people know you exist. I go back on the green and completely castigate the latest tranny to show her pedo ass and all my favorite streamers are online like I never left.

I do a bunch of adult shit like go to 7/11 and download job application forms and research the split-second developments in the crypto pipeline and I line up some Widowmaker anal and life is good, you know? I'm eating healthier, I'm trying Gatorade, Sprite, even Coke and Pepsi like some kind of PETAcuck estrogen VeggieTales health freak. I'm watching Widowmaker's rubbery purple pussy stretch around a huge dong. I don't know if it's intentional but the way they make the video, I can imagine that it's my own penis. I try to jerk off but I fall asleep. Her long legs criss-cross like they do when you're spectating a Widow, high heel bug movements, and sometimes that curl when she grapples away and tucks her body in and pops up, that nice little leap before you fall down to the spot you grappled to. I could never figure her rifle out, but in my dream, it's headshot every time. Dancing around, waggling my rifle and scoping in and crouching tight and I watch the meter charge up and I blow out the brains of the perfectly arranged shooting gallery of minorities on the enemy team, all the countries of the world, Pixar special ed forced inclusion first bipolar Italian faggot to have a female penis. Drop my spider mine and listen to it hiss and pop behind me so I grapple again but I miss and fall down and I panic shoot but my rifle is like jello and I'm out of ammo and—

I wake up and my boxers are sticky and I'm freaking out. It feels like a wet dream but it's everywhere. I stand up and look inside and there's this green stuff pooling around my balls. I calm down and take a few breaths and I start pulling my boxers off and that's when I feel it tugging on my body hair. In my head, I hear my mom complaining to her hugbox womblet friends about how much it hurts getting waxed. I can't get my boxers off because the goop is sticking to my ass and it feels connected to the inside of my body. I feel really nauseous, then it oozes out like a big rope of syrup and clings to the back of my leg.

I'm in my room 24/7 again, like DiCaprio in that movie where he invents the perfect plane the globalists don't want him to have because it can go on water. My dad loved that movie. I know if I hustle my dad will love me too. I keep the bottles under my bed but there's too many and they're everywhere now. I don't know how to explain the crazy of seeing the sun shine through my toxic green anal secretions in the morning. When you see a gallon bottle of Mountain Dew full of something that came from your ass, it changes a guy.

I start posting again. I feel a little more sane every time I see that arrow pointing at each sentence, making it the perfect color. I do some pickup games to help me get back into male socialization and I guess I joke a lot about how I'm going to fucking KMS if I don't drink Mountain Dew every second of the day and we take it to Discord and it's like yeah this is an issue people struggle with. Justin, the guy I heal for, he's a good listener, we've been chatting for a while now so I feel like I can tell him shit. Apparently the group I play with has a place over in Hayward where they do esports training and talk about serious issues like this, like real nofap purification fix your life Greco-Roman get that bread shit.

He says internet contagion stuff like this happens a lot and goes over different mental illness and personality quizzes with me and we talk about the soda thing again and he asks if I love sugar because that's a possible symptom. I cry as I type, *i love sugar.* I'm PMSing so hard. I need to get out of this house because I think my mom's estrogen is affecting me like an environmental pollutant, probably in most things I touch. I shouldn't have eaten those Luna bars. I try to remember how many Luna bars I ate and I start panicking. But as I pack my shit, I start to feel calmer. I know what the problem is and I'm getting out.

The house is kind of in the hills, in a shady part with lots of trees. I shake hands with Justin. This is the first time I've actually hung out with these guys IRL. I can see I got sweat on his hand but he doesn't say anything about it. I see the other guys on the team and even some girls, some 7s and 7.5s which has me feeling like, okay maybe these guys are legit, even though I think one of them is a trap. He shows me around the property and I see some real nice trees with lots of bark and I touch them and get sap on my fingers, so I ask where the bathroom is. He says sure, right down the hall, and goes back to playing Smash in the living room with the others all chugging soda and having a great time.

I stare at the sink. I want to clean my sticky hand but just touching the knob is like radioactive ice. Then I laugh because it's all in my head and I turn on the sink and run nice clean water through my fingers.

I trip out of the bathroom and try to tell them the water is bad, maybe you need your water checked, and Justin is saying, hey, calm down, what's up, you need anything?

I say, Mountain fucking Dew, please and thank you.

He brings me a can and snaps the tab for me and I feel so grateful. I'm shaking so hard I cut my lip on the sharp metal edge. Blood and Mountain Dew trickles down my chin, dripping on my hoodie. Fuck, I say, looking down so my face almost disappears into the hoodie. I feel shrunk down and pathetic. He brings me a bandaid but I can't figure out how to put a bandaid on my mouth, so I just sit there and bleed, crying a little.

He says, what's going on, man? He wears a hoodie like me so maybe he gets it, maybe I can explain things to him. But his hair is kind of long so I say, you're not a boymoder, right? You're not one of them, are you? I can see he's getting a weird look so I say, just kidding, haha. Gimme a sec and I'll be out.

I'm on the bathroom floor and the tile is nice and cold under my face. The can of Dew spilled everywhere. I watch the ants come for it until the puddle of soda is fuzzy and black. The door opens and Justin is like shit, you're still in here?

I say something but I don't think it comes out super clear. The ants crawl past my face and I think I'm hypnotized.

I got you, he says, holding a bottle of Dew to my mouth, safe plastic that won't cut me. I suck on it and my lips crinkle up like I'm going to cry. He supports my head with his hand and helps me finish the 20oz bottle. My stomach hurts, this swollen bump visible even under my hoodie, too heavy to move. I can't remember the last time I pissed, I think I have a kidney infection. The others are crowding into the bathroom and whispering and I get scared they're going to call an ambulance and I say I'm not on insurance. They look down and their hair falls on my face. It itches and I turn my head and my face is in the soda puddle and it's black with ants and I'm coughing and spitting them out and I try to stand up and I slip on the soda and bang my head. I just need to use the fucking bathroom. Get the fuck. Get the fuck out.

I dream about Widowmaker but her skin is green and she's crawling all over me. I always thought she'd taste like Playdoh but what comes out is acid and it burns and I try to get away and I wake up and there's dirt everywhere and it's night.

I stand up and almost scream, falling back on my knees. I'm cramping so bad I feel like I might actually explode if I get up. I try crawling and my belly drags on the dirt. I'm so skinny it feels like my stomach is going to break off and roll away. I'm panting like crazy.

That's when I realize, I'm naked. I reach out trying to find my hoodie and my phone and something rattles under my fingers and I almost shit myself. Just a bunch of plastic bottles rolling around. I curl up on my side and look for the moon or stars or even a single street light but there's nothing but dirt. I must have walked into the hills, walked really far. I start panicking thinking about those news stories about people who didn't respect nature and went for a hike and fucking died. I just want to see my favorite streamers and check my sites, all that simple stupid stuff. I just want to know people are alive in the world and something is going on somewhere. I'd even settle for some crickets but I can't hear a single bug, which is really scary. Maybe I fell in an old mine shaft, those places no one can hear you and they never find you and you die. Minecraft is so fucking scary. I put my arms over my face and try to breathe but it's really hard. Please fucking help me, okay? The kind of thing you say even if you never say it. Please fucking help me.

Need to drink something. I remember that. You can live without food for weeks but you need liquids or you die. I'll drink dirty puddle water, I don't care. I check the bottles, rolling away the empties so I won't keep checking the same ones but soon I'm holding the last one and trying not to panic. I sniff it even though it won't change anything, just feels like the only thing I can do to get a single familiar detail in this darkness.

Mountain Dew.

Something creaks like a tree and my heart goes crazy. If there's a tree, I'm not in a mine shaft. I walked here and I can walk back. I just need to shit and I'll be able to walk and I won't die and I'll be alive. I groan and roll back onto my stomach. I push hard on my fragging arm, weighted mouse, I can do this. I'm almost on my feet when the worst pain I ever experienced stabs my abs and my face hits the ground.

The creaking gets louder, scarier, then I see light. I think someone has a flashlight up on that hill, so I say hey, all dehydrated and croaky. Hey. Help me. Please.

Justin comes down the hill. Creak. Creak. Creak. It's a stairway. Door glowing at the top. He puts his hand on my belly and it's scraped so raw from dragging in the dirt that I can feel every line on his palm.

Hhhlp, I say.

The others are here too, hair hanging over me again, eyes black and shiny. I try to crawl away but every inch is raping me inside. I think I'm actually going to die.

Justin whispers to me and I can't understand what he's saying, but his voice is relaxing and steady like the callouts he'd do in-game. His girlfriend touches my face and her hair smells like flowers and candy. Another girl is holding her phone up and watching something, a movie about aliens, found footage, shaky light on dirt, then I realize the pale green boy on the ground is me, my hair encrusted with Dew and hanging over my face so only one eye is visible, big and wide and scared. There's so much soda staining me that multiple generations of ants and flies are dead in the slimy crust. I'm surrounded by bottles. I can't see my dick, tiny and scared behind my swollen stomach. The pits behind my knees are pooling with sweat. Justin's arm enters the screen stroking my back so lightly that the little hairs on my tailbone stand up and I get ASMR shivers.

Honeydew time, the girl (trap) says, still filming, so I keep my head down so my hair covers my face so I won't become a meme. Give me my phone, I say, face burning so hot I can't breathe. Give me my fucking phone. Something sloshes inside me and my face grinds into the dirt and all I can do is moan and cry as syrup squirts from my asshole. But there's no relief, just slow, aching oozing, sticky green ropes hanging so heavy from my ass it feels like my asshole is going to tear off, sticking to my balls and foreskin and hanging between my thighs.

I crawl toward the stairs, screaming every slur I can think of, telling them I called the cops, telling them someone is coming to save me. Every time I move, syrup pumps out of me, sticky on my calves and feet. I get my elbows on the first step and it hurts but I haul myself up, belly smacking onto the wood, dragging through splinters.

Justin puts a 2-liter bottle of Dew on the step. It's so big and green like a beautiful alien crystal, realer than everything else. It's like I'm in a commercial. His hand rests on my tailbone and I feel like I need to piss or shit. The tingling is so bad I'm going crazy.

Don't do that, I say. You fucking faggot.

Shut the fuck up, Clyde, you fucking faggot, he says, and my name isn't Clyde, I don't get it, but everyone laughs and their hair drowns me again, that long female hair with the nice shampoo, and the thick doomer hair in tangles and curls. I get schizo goosebumps all over and my spine feels like it's melting through my asshole. I lunge up another step but slide back down, landing hard on my belly. It feels like my balls were kicked, except my balls are my entire body. It hurts so bad I can barely see.

I feel plastic in my mouth. The ridged rim of the bottle. I push my tongue against it but it fills my mouth and my cheeks puff out so I try to swallow and get a few gulps down but it doesn't stop and it shoots up through my nose and bursts from the sides of my mouth all over my face into my eyes blinding me and it flows back into my nose where Dew is already coming out. He keeps the bottle in my mouth, heavy as a bowling ball, until all 2 liters have drained through my face.

It's calm after, like the calm you get after vomiting. The Dew cools on my face, eyes stuck shut. Sugary snot drips down the back of my throat. Every breath smells like stomach acid and corn syrup. I feel little tickles which must have been ant scouts because soon they're crawling up my legs and across my face. I don't move. If I move it hurts. I feel the pressure growing down there but the slime is so thick and slow it hardens to a plug. My guts are like a kinked up hose full of syrup, backed up to my stomach, bubbling up my throat, blasting my sinuses, then dripping back down my throat, over and over, soda and stomach acid. Sometimes a tooth breaks apart, and I swallow it. My mouth is so smooth now. I never open my eyes because all I'll see is swollen skin that wasn't meant to stretch that far, stretch marks like a fucking cow.

The only thing that helps is when they come down and tickle me with their hair and fingers, and my stomach tingles and the syrup plug loosens enough for my guts to start spurting into whatever plastic container they're holding out. APHID BOY GAMER SYRUP someone says, and Justin looks at me with his shiny black eyes and his hair stiff and clicking and he tells me how much it helps the team, they just made championships, and he promises to tell me about the big plays, and every time I think it's finally over, his fingers brush that little patch of hair at the base of my spine and my ass spits like a squirt gun and a big cable of syrup shoots out, hips aching, so intense my lips rip open the mask of corn syrup and bleed, the only thing I ever taste besides sugar and artificial flavors, and I gag through the sweet blood and try to say the few words I have time to say before the gallon bottle stuffs my mouth. Each time I try to remember what words I said before so I can say different words that might work this time. But their hands just stroke my belly as it swells up again.

that they shall drive thee from men, and thy dwelling shall be with the beasts of the field, and they shall make thee to eat grass as oxen, and they shall wet thee with the dew of heaven

ELF 9/11

Elf guys dripping cum in the cages of Ground Zero
We pump the cum into a reservoir under 9/11
We gotta get their foreskins too
No questions asked.

It isn't my job to criticize the program
My job is to stockpile the biggest quantity of elf
cum in this country since World War 2
And I will stop at nothing
That's why I'm authorized to cry.

We bored a hole directly at the center of 9/11
Calculated according to the most precise psycho-
geographic accuracies.
The great one will put his dick there
To send two beams of light into the sky
For obvious reasons.

There is a unique mineral formed only at Ground Zero, at the singular and heady confluence of a crashed passenger plane: steel beams, jet fuel, building parts, building powders, and what we are allowed to refer to only in euphemism as Hero Dust. Did you know there was a special temperature reached only by the unique conditions of 9/11 due to the incredible conflux of wind conditions, architectural and avionic parts only in use during that era, MPH of the plane, etc? You also need that. It's so unique. So singular. So heady.

This mineral is called Eagle's Tears. it's a vital component of elf cum refraction. we make them wear it to energize their load. it weighs like 10,000 pounds due to hyperdensity, so we have to rip out all their bones and replace them with steel beams. Anyways, they gave me a little shard of Eagle Tears as a thank you very much for my service.

I get clawmarks from the elf guys
But it's okay
I go to Applebees to sit in a booth for an hour
Screaming silently at myself
I order nothing.
I can't ejaculate inside my wife anymore.

You know the iceberg meme? You're a smart kid, of course you do...
They've got one of those up north. except without the meme part.

The toxins of 9/11 are frozen in this iceberg
Carried by wind currents.
Me and the guys go there sometimes on vacation.
It's a black site for elf guys and things get a little crazy sometimes
But it's cool

There's a reason they're called human rights
Not elf rights

Goddamn elves looking at my dick 24/7 when I'm sunbathing on the ice caps

They got em crucified on those special non-invasive humane magnetic crucifiers

goddamn i keep getting these headaches

hhhh

huuuaaah

i grip my Eagle's Tear for comfort and it cuts my hand.
it looks just like spraypainted metal.

the sun is so bright out here
beams off the ice caps fit to blind you.

but it gets less bright every year
soon i won't have to wear sunglasses
and i can stare at the new earth god is creating under the ice
with my own eyes

CUNT
TOWARD
ENEMY

Everything is an explosive. Every thought is a sort of explosion inside the head. When you give me your hand I feel as if something is exploding inside you.

— Karel Čapek, *Krakatit*

Don't move.

The LED screens and billboards around the Fuchsia World Mall all say the same thing.

People run, of course.

The parking lot explodes. The mall shakes. Smoke rises from the courtyard at the center, or traps itself dark behind cracked windows.

Eventually, people stop moving. Some have the presence of mind to understand what's happening, the rest get lucky with shock and concussion, or the inability to move with their new bodies. The border is delineated by horrified bystanders, clean and unharmed, except for the powderized city drifting into the creases of their clothes and lungs.

Lazur drives into the storm of carcinogens, windshield growing grayer. The smell of almonds, even half a mile away. A tribute to classical plastic explosives, Nobel 808s, and so much more than heartbreak.

Lazur parks his car. Rental, because things could always get worse. His second-best jacket, and the shirt he fell asleep in last night. Dark hair slashed with early white, and blue undertones when the sun hits it.

Car alarms are still going off like crickets of death. The almond cloy is overwhelming this close. At least it deodorizes the bodies.

He shows his badge, dropping it twice. His fingers shouldn't be this sweaty already.

"He asked for you."

"He's alive?"

But even as Lazur says it, he knows. Or they would have asked for a bomb technician closer than a six-hour drive. This is a very personal terrorist incident.

He finishes his milk tea and crushes the cup in his hand. He's about to drop it then remembers the cameras. It might look tough, rolling up the sleeves kind of deal, or it could come off as disrespectful. And littering is littering. There's already been enough of that today. Sneakers, sole detached like a skin flap. A handheld console, translucent purple plastic shattered into rare earth blood minerals. A wedding ring, perfectly lodged in a crack of the parking lot, like it was lost for years and years and years.

His phone buzzes and he almost pisses himself. Through the cracked screen, over the wallpaper of him and his mother at Olive Garden, a notification hovers.

You're safe for one minute.

He walks past frozen people sitting on the ground, or standing with aching legs, afraid to even kneel. Their eyes follow him. Waxwork museum of 21st century parking lot life. Authentic explosions included.

How does it work? Motion sensors, toggled off? In which case, he could try to save some of these people. Tell them to run.

But if it's manual, human eyes reflecting security monitors, then that is a very bad idea.

Facial recognition would be cute. The one face that won't blow up the mall. How special.

He walks past a crater, heat radiating through his sneakers. The blasted asphalt is like volcanic rock.

The mall is a cathedral of ice, reverberating with industrial aircon. The screens are playing commercials again, and the actors' wide smiles have a desperate, hostage taint to them.

In the mall's courtyard, black sloughing waterfalls of structural gore. People stare down silently, more waxworks. A mother grips her toddler like she's going to crush him, trying to keep this panicking nascent mind from reacting normally to terror and setting off the nearest bomb, wherever it is.

Someone is still breathing in the fragments of that heavy mall pot, covered in plastic leaves and fake soil like he dug out of his own grave. Survived the initial blast, but fortunately for his neighbors, he's lost too much blood to thrash. He just writhes slowly like a worm, under the threshold of the bomb sensor.

There it is. Like a dead pixel.

A black box.

This is the bomb. The one that matters. The others were just setting the stage.

Video screens drain of their commercials, happy families and pristine cars fading to black. An unfamiliar voice echoes through the speakers. But a familiar way of saying it.

"There's enough to send you to the moon."

The screens turn back on. Grainy feed, but it doesn't matter at that scale.

Lazur doesn't recognize him at first. Broken in a wheelchair. Drooling out the side of a ruptured jaw.

Rubicon could make a very mean, very reasonable bomb from household parts by age ten. They flocked to his fingers like doves.

Money in the blood. Took his final exams at the atrocity. Flying colors, blood in the clouds. Arms dealt like hands. You know idiot savants? Imagine that, but really smart, with no downsides. His car bombs purred like a luxury sedan. Magazine spread, the blond bombshell. Hottest heirs under 30. He burnt up.

Lazur tilts his head back, forced to look up at the twisted body replicated on every screen. "Can you hear me?"

The shredded mouth moves after only a slight delay. "Yes." Lazur wonders if they can trace the transmission. Probably. But not in time.

He says, "You look great."

Rubicon laughs, exposing the strain on his remaining lung. The mall-wide sound system catches every bit of grit, an auditory microscope into fried tissue and bone shrapnel.

"It's my twenty-first birthday." Rubicon tips back a mini-bottle, brown liquor pouring through the holes in his face.

Lazur looks at the bomb, that unadorned black box like an alien interpretation of gift giving. "I didn't get you anything."

"I disagree." The screens turn off, leaving error messages tall as trees. Rubicon's voice jumps to the bomb, suddenly smaller, fragile, intimate. "Why don't you take a look. I'm kind of proud of it."

Natural light falls on the bomb from the open ceiling of the courtyard, cold bright afternoon tempered by clouds. He wonders if it's going to rain. Probably. But not the way you like to see.

"Can I wear a bomb suit?"

Silence, susurrus with the dead air of Rubicon's feed. "Sure. Let's embrace the ritual."

He walks back to the parking lot. As they bring out the bomb suit, a weakness enters his legs. He puts his hands on a car hood and bows his head like he's thinking deep heroic thoughts, but really just trying not to fall to the ground like a scared child. Coming back out was the wrong move. It triggered a false sense of visceral relief, tricked his body into thinking he survived it, when he hasn't even begun. The black box is still there, unopened, fissile with secrets.

Everyone is watching him. So he goes back inside.

The bomb suit weighs 85 pounds. It was comforting the first time he put it on. Everyone wants armor. But now it feels heavy as his soul.

People keep talking at him. Texts, emails, calls. He knows they can't give him anything he needs. No amount of research, protocol, international expertise, tech specs, or cutting-edge tools can change the outcome. He silences his phone, then swivels, taking in the mall like a deep sea diver. All bombs render their surroundings alien. Not just after, but before. Alone with this secret pressure. Inside the veil of its inverted explosion. Before a great noise, great silence.

The suit doesn't help with the alienation. A bulbous carapace that destroys all definition of his body, like those projections of what humans will look like evolved for cars after millions of years. Bomb world neanderthal.

Someone clears their throat. A woman on the floor, dark matter drying on her jeans. She holds out a tablet.

Lazur stares at her through the spacesuit.

It's for you, she says in a dehydrated voice, but with some dignity, a subdued spirit of offense.

"Thanks," he says, not sure if she heard him. He wishes he could comfort her. Take off the helmet and talk like normal people. No. Emotion has a specific atmospheric cost inside this sweltering suit. He can't afford to be soft. Because humans were not meant to commune with bombs. Beasts of nitrogen, hexamine demons, plastic deities that slowly and instantly invade reality. He has to be a device.

He takes the tablet. Rubicon looks up at him through the faint smears of the woman's fingers. Tracks of her daily use: compulsively scrolling her socials, tapping at gacha rewards, gripping the edges to position herself in the best light for friends, family, a lover.

"How much time do I have?"

"Look at the bomb. Then maybe I'll tell you."

Lazur trudges to the black case. He'd hoped that a closer look would reveal new details, but it remains surprisingly minimalist compared to Rubicon's past work. He can't see a way inside the monolithic form, it resists his touch, his interpretation. Maybe it's a joke. A combustible koan.

"Is there a timer?"

"Of course. You need to stay motivated. But it's not the point."

"Then what is?"

"Funny you'd say that."

Lazur sweats, trapped with his own body heat. It's only going to get hotter. If the suit had holes, it wouldn't be protective.

Rubicon says, "Take the suit off."

"I think it looks good. Kind of suave and sexy."

"It won't help you. Not with the ordinance I'm using."

He leans against the bomb, propped up by his own death, cooking in the wearable sauna, dizzy, dizzying, dizzier.

"I've established that you have nothing to gain with the suit. And you'll be more dexterous."

The crip fuck is right. The suit is a comfort object. A stuffed animal. He needs to expose himself, oxygenate his organs. Because the only way out is with his head. He rips the front plate off the suit, getting a blast of that cool mall air. Plastic buckles click and release their black straps, and his armor crumbles around him.

He breaks his kit out. His spudger. Wire cutters. Hex key. Hemostat. Cold chisel, made of beryllium copper to avoid sparking.

"That won't help either. It's solid state. Pure failsafe."

Lazur believes him. Rubicon tired long ago of the usual games. His last bomb was a gauntlet, taking Lazur on a sweaty tour through explosive history. Black powder, nitroglycerin, gelignite, dynamite, vintage plastic. A sample platter, a gift basket, a greatest hits anthology. It was almost interesting, after a career of defusing the same entry-level pipe bombs and garden-variety plastic explosives.

The point is, Rubicon doesn't repeat himself. A pivot to minimalism makes sense.

Lazur runs his hand across the case. Smooth, well-machined, betraying nothing. Then he walks around the bomb, and finally sees it. A hole. Like a large headphone jack.

Maybe it emits something. A gas? That would reach a wide area.

He shines a penlight inside. The interior is coated with some kind of rubber. There's a fissure at the end made of a similar polymer, a smaller hole within the hole.

"Move the tablet."

"What?" Snapping. Irritated.

"So I can see you."

Lazur picks up the tablet. He thinks about tossing it over the railing. But it would be a pointless defiance. And with how much Rubicon is talking, maybe there's a negotiation angle after all. Or maybe the shattered anatomy just makes him look vulnerable. Unless the blast scrambled his brain, this is the same person, with the same choice of weapons. Except both are obfuscated, skin as inscrutable as this bomb.

Lazur places the tablet against the glass railing. “Do I get anything for that?”

“I’m not the Nintendo Power hotline. That’s what people your age used, right?”

“I don’t play games.”

Crackling laughter that turns to wet coughing. “I thought I’d get to use this body more. Or I never thought of it at all. Same thing.”

Rubicon spits, a messy, pathetic dribble down his chin, too weak to clear his own face. Saliva drips off-screen. The background is painted black. No hints to location. But probably in the same state, judging by latency.

“I had a dream I was kissing someone. On a roller coaster. The roller coaster wasn’t moving. It was inside a mall. Maybe that’s why I chose the location.”

“It’s a nice public place. Lots of people.”

“See. You get me.”

Shrug.

“I woke up and my face hurt. I keep forgetting what shape it is now. I realized I’d never kiss anyone again. After a certain point of ablation, it’s just meat slapping against meat.”

“I didn’t do that to you.”

"When you raided me, I was on a three-day coke bender, up all night in my workshop. I panicked. My finger moved an inch to the left. I don't have that finger anymore."

"How do you know I was there?"

"Because my bombs didn't go off. The ones that were supposed to protect me."

"I'm not the only defusal expert in the world."

"You knew what to look for. You get my sense of humor."

"I was just one person, doing my job."

"If it was just that. I could forgive you. But you weren't just a hapless little technician bumbling along. I think you showed them where I was."

Lazur doesn't answer.

"You could feel it, couldn't you? In the guts of my last bomb. I was too forensically generous. Not enough details sanded off, too many exotic, traceable ingredients. I overshared. I was just so excited to finally have an audience that could understand me."

"Looking at it made me sick."

Excitement breaks through Rubicon's fractured face, facets of flushed skin. "Really? I wish I could have shown you the other one. The night you came. There's still pieces of it inside me."

Lazur slaps his hands on the black box. "I want to know about this one."

"You know how it goes. The payload is transformed into highly concentrated, high-pressure gas. It expands, violently out of sync with the surrounding atmosphere. Shock wave. Debris rains for miles. Radiation—"

"It's a dirty bomb?"

"The dirtiest."

Lazur picks through his tools. Blank. Nothing. Useless.

"It's beautiful how such a tiny quantity of materials can blight so much land, for so long. Dominating the chromosomes of our fellow man."

Lazur doesn't respond.

"Can you hear me?"

"I'm going to find the room you're hiding in, and I'm going to shoot you." And all the bombs will unvomit themselves, and all the people will come back together.

“Maybe.” The lazy word hangs there. Rubicon doesn’t need to say anything else. The bomb is right there, total and commanding.

“You could have done something with your life.”

“Shut up, dad. This is what I’m good at.”

“Blowing people up isn’t a career—”

“It created your career.”

“Bombs kill—”

“Bombs equalize.”

“Another victory for democracy.”

“Tired macho quips won’t get you out of this.”

“I feel tired.” He thought Rubicon’s death, supposed death, would end it. But every suspicious bag on the subway was full of fear, his pores rewired to pump rookie sweat, virginal trembling in his wire cutters.

“You look tired.”

4th of July, on a date, baseball at night, the sky full of burning worms, popping and crackling with their consumption of the air, their gnashing of bismuth trioxide. How could fireworks be that loud, were they always that loud? Surrounded by thousands of mannequins, cheers blasting from loudspeakers. He excused himself to the stadium bathroom and hid inside a stall, finishing his beer in quick, automatic swallows. It tasted like aftermath. He walked home, lost, unable to find the way back to his seat. She never texted him back.

"You eating okay?"

Potato chips. Moldy takeout. An insidious lack of appetite. As if waiting for something massive and inorganic, pica for rubble.

"I could order you a pizza—"

"Are you fucking me here?"

"Huh?"

Lazur grabs the tablet. "Is there a point to trying, or not?"

Rubicon leans back in his wheelchair, a defensive posture, or simply too weak to keep his spine erect. "There is a point. If you can find it."

Lazur kneels down, trying to feel under the bomb. Flush with the floor on every side.

Rubicon says, "How are you since the whole explosion thing? I feel like we have so much to catch up on."

"Fine. Just beautiful."

"You're not with that one lady anymore."

"That's not your business."

"You probably brought home too much baggage. So tense. When's this guy gonna explode?"

"I never hit anyone."

"Would you hit me?"

Hitting wouldn't be enough. If his fist touched that face, he wouldn't be able to pull it back. It would spread. Digging in. Something prolonged, animalistic. And it would be so easy. He can see exactly where each bone was fused back together. A grafted, cannibalized body, forced to eat itself. Thigh sculpted into face. Hips into cheekbones. The boy would shatter. And all this would end. Fingers around his neck, no, there's no need for traditional weak points. You can break him anywhere. Hook your thumbs into the wet corners of his mouth. Set your nails to the sockets of his eyes. Soft shell crab. He would beg if you got close. No screen to hide behind. Feeling the fear in his whole body. How completely helpless he is. His soul, his capacity for thought, trapped inside a fragile frame that can barely survive his own heartbeat.

Even Lazur's tongue is enough to crush him. It'll have to do for now. "I'd worry more about your own state of mind. Leaving a pathetic mess like this for me to clean up."

"It's not a mess. I worked very hard, very carefully, on every detail—" Spit catches in his throat and he coughs up pink saliva, a drop hitting the screen.

"Choking on me?"

Rubicon wipes his face. "I could ask the same thing."

"You didn't give me anything to work with. This is just a nihilistic fuck me."

"It's not." Rubicon sounds like he was accused of faking his homework. He leans forward in the wheelchair, and Lazur sees it. The marionette torture in the boy's spine, the wrists too weak to stabilize without pain. It must have taken many painstaking hours to make whatever this bomb is. He looks like he's going to say something else, but he just hangs there, shivering with neuralgia.

"I know," Lazur says quietly.

"I think a lot. About what I make."

"You're good at it."

Lazur's eternal instinct. Don't let it blow up. Things or people. The slightest vibration of molecules can lead to an irreversible and shocking outcome.

Rubicon hangs his head, letting the saliva drip until he can talk. When he does, a strand of clear drool hangs from his tattered lip. "Thanks?"

"But it's not enough. Not after what happened to you."

Silence from the tablet.

"You can't catch up anymore."

Wet rasp. "Can you?"

"I have a real job. Helping people. Not blow up. I believe in something—"

"Sure. Casimir Pulaski with wire cutters."

"Fuck you."

Rubicon assumes a posture that might once have been insouciance, but now comes off as muscle memory for a body that no longer exists. He reaches off-screen and Lazur hears the click of a keyboard.

The mall screens turn on. A red countdown.

Fifteen minutes.

It doesn't matter what he does here. The elements of cheap, scalable annihilation have entered this reality. Bombs blowing through the world like storm clouds.

He thinks of the soul that enters each bomb, to act as its detonator, some vital link in the mechanism. Surrendering to this bright new form as it explodes from the hyper-flagellating vest around your chest.

Trading a dim, anonymous, interminable life for a single brilliant inversion of your hell.

We are in a labyrinth and the string that leads us out is a wire.

Rubicon leans forward. A scrap of blond hair falls over his eyes and he forks it to the side with his fingers. “Did you mean it?”

“Mean what?”

“That I’m good. At what I do.”

Lazur thinks of the delicate mechanisms he balanced his very sweat against, rapt with surgical flow. “Sure.”

Rubicon looks away, then his head jerks back, the scar tissue on his neck restraining him like a collar. “I’m a little embarrassed now. It’s a different kind of bomb.”

“Different?”

“It’s not as sophisticated as the others I made for you. It’s just. Different.”

“Okay.”

“I’m still good at music. I’m just trying a new instrument.”

"Got it. No judgment. I'll leave that for the war crime tribunal."

"Thanks."

You lie motionless in an ocean of immeasurable, unanalyzable, unutilized forces; you are surrounded not by the walls of the room, quiet people and the rustling branches of trees, but by an ammunition store, a cosmic magazine prepared for the most frightful deed. You tap matter with your finger as if you were testing casks of ekrasite to see if they are full.

— Karel Čapek, *Krakatit*

Lazur stares at the bomb. It yields nothing. He feels like he's going crazy.

"What did you mean, different?"

"Uh. Most of it is incredibly powerful explosive. No surprise. Packed very tight. Very dense. The rest is diagnostic machinery."

"Diagnostic?"

"You won't need your tools for this. Well. Maybe your tool. In the vernacular sense."

"What the fuck."

"The bomb disarms when it receives your DNA in seminal form."

"Fuck off."

"Come on, Lazur. Your biological clock is ticking. Haha."

"I have to stick my dick in some kid's edgy freshman art project—"

Rubicon reaches for the webcam, and for the first time Lazur notices his pinkie and ring finger are missing. The camera swoops over the keloid canyons and emaciated valleys of his flesh. "You think anyone is ever going to look at this body and think of me as a kid ever again?"

Fourteen minutes.

"I know. A real boner killer."

Hostages whisper like jealous statues. Lazur leans over the bomb, eyes shut. It smells like chemicals. Workshop taint. A whiff of almond.

Rubicon rests his hand on the arm of the wheelchair. His thumb is missing too. "What's the play, Laz?"

Lazur runs his finger around the bomb's hole. Maybe he can jerk off instead. Push his cum inside—

"I thought of everything. You have to physically nut in the bomb."

Hostages sit in front of a Build-a-Bear. One of them has a dark stain down the front of his pants. He stares at Lazur, or maybe he's just dissociating.

"Remember. The first part of fucking a bomb is acceptance."

"You didn't give me enough time."

"A red-blooded patriot like you should have no problem fucking a bomb."

"You don't know what color my blood is."

"A watery translucent effluvia. Microplastics and ennui."

"Damn." Lazur watches the red numbers change, huge and important like some event he couldn't possibly have anything to do with. He wants to be one of the people waiting for him to fix this.

"I know you'll do it," the ruined mouth says.

Lazur covers his face, breathing through sweaty palms.

"Because you're the best."

Lazur goes into a shop and drags out cardboard cutouts. Anime girl with insectile sword, exoskeletoned star marine, some kind of edgy furry mascot. He never played any of those games. They're just some dumb shit he never learned about and probably never will.

He positions them around the bomb. A startling sound comes from the tablet. He flinches, then realizes it was Rubicon laughing. Like someone trying to play a smashed violin.

"You're really going to do it?"

Lazur seethes. His lower half is hidden from the Build-A-Bear refugees. And the hostage panopticon, are they really going to assume he's fucking the bomb? Fucking perverts. Dick hawks circling overhead. No. It's probably not the first thing that comes to mind. He just has to, there, unzip, snake it through, keep his pants on. He leans on the bomb all casual, like he's about to eat his lunch. Just a working stiff. Hopefully.

Thirteen minutes. Rubicon's wet mouth noise through the tablet like out of sync hentai foley. Still soft. He tucks himself back in and zips his fly.

"Giving up?"

In a Hot Topic next to the cash register, he finds a small half-used bottle of warm lotion.

"Good idea. I didn't make it self-lubricating."

"Frigid bitch."

Another laugh. That busted xylophone of teeth, a single lung's worth of air, and the tongue, bright and pink and intact, struggling not to fall out of the mouth.

All bravado aside, he doesn't feel good. He just needed to feel like he wasn't helpless, so he did those things, without emotion, to shut that kid up. But now he's here. The pop culture cutouts surround him like a praetorian guard. The lotion sits on the bomb, a strand of hair smeared on the side. How long was it laying lukewarm and stale, soothing the eczema of a teen cashier?

He unzips again. The tip of his cock brushes the rubber rim of the hole. He wonders what it feels like inside. Chop off his dick. Spew acid. Roast him like a sausage.

Is that really Rubicon's style? He likes big explosions. Or he did. His artistic direction has clearly changed. After all, he lived through a blast. Felt it intimately in his muscles, bones, nerves. How deeply was his mental process transformed?

"Better pop before my bomb does."

"Don't talk."

"They call it total body disruption. The thing a bomb does. Chunks. Gibs. Meat cloud. I was in awe when I read the term. Twelve years old."

Lazur closes his eyes, trying to regulate his breathing.

"What are you thinking about? What's your go-to?"

He scans for mental images, desperately flipping through obscene fantasies tracing all the way back to puberty.

"You probably need ol' reliable for this one. The stuff that gets you off when you need to fall asleep."

Get out of my head, you fuck.

Rubicon says, "You know the first thing I jerked off to?"

"They didn't mention it in the briefing."

"The first thing I ever jerked off to was Kajaki."

"I didn't think anyone else saw it."

"Yeah. You never meet anyone who saw it."

"They can't handle the circus."

"Halfway through I started laughing and couldn't stop. I felt like I was going crazy."

This stupid conversation is the only thing keeping him from freezing up. So he allows himself to speak naturally, aimlessly, knowing he needs to relax on the deepest level. "I always wanted to see it again. I don't know why. It made me so sad."

"We should watch it together sometime."

Lazur fingers the mouth of the bomb. Feels soft enough. "Dirty bomb," he whispers.

"What?"

Dirty little bomb...

"Krakatit, Krakatoa, Kajaki, kraken, Krakus...death is in the K's...the STOP...the voiceless velar plosive... are you voiceless, Lazur? Or plosive?"

"Please be quiet. I'm trying to concentrate."

"Maybe I lied. Maybe I went small and cozy. Packed it so you'll survive. So you can be like me."

Lazur shudders, a gruesome, slimy dread coating every inch of his skin. Eleven minutes. He jerks off in small, weak, scared motions, part of him still trying to preserve his dignity even as he grinds against his death.

"I made the interior extra nice for you. I didn't want you to have a hard time in front of all these people."

"Right. Then the razors come out, and the scorpions."

"It's not a fucking Saw trap. This is medical-grade silicone."

"Fucking ridiculous."

"Did you go inside? Was that you going inside?"

"So fucking stupid."

"Look around. Then tell me how stupid this is."

The dead bodies do lend an air of gravitas. Lazur presses flush against the bomb, trying to conceal his penetration. He gasps at the tight, sticky sensation of his cock embedded in a high-yield, block-leveling explosive.

"Why are you doing this?"

"I'd already tested your technical strength, took you through the intellectual games—"

"It wasn't a game to me."

"If you wanted to help people, you could have become a plumber. A nursing home aid. A shit scrubber."

Lazur pushes a little deeper, trying to relax. The bomb hasn't cut his dick off yet.

"But you became a bomb technician. You headed straight for the alien apparatus, the archonic convergence of it all. The screaming edge of the future."

With his cock soft in the interior of a doomsday device, Lazur feels the sudden urge to beg. Hey, turn off the bomb. Please? For the sake of whatever delusion you've invested in me.

"You were the only one who understood. All that effort that dissipates into nothing—"

Ten minutes. His head pounds with blood, the wrong one. "Tell me about the bomb. Help me understand." As long as Rubicon is still on the line, the fantasy of negotiation is alive. Someone who can end the nightmare, even if he won't.

"I wanted to make something high-concept. A blockbuster hit for the masses."

"An accessible bomb for your average guy."

"I think everyone watching will get it."

Lazur thrusts faster, fighting to keep his half-erection alive. "I'm just a low-concept guy in a high-concept world."

"You're a component in my bomb now."

Lazur freezes. Wondering if he's fucking his way to some kind of ironic twist.

"Don't worry. You can be an off switch. If you believe in yourself. And uh, fuck the bomb real good."

Grind grind grind. His foreskin pinches. He adjusts it. Squirts more lotion on. Still not hard enough. He always jerked off with TV in the background. He needs a distraction. "So you've just been convalescing this whole time?"

"My dad left me a lot of money."

"I hate guys like that. Letting their kids grow up to be narcissists."

"What kind of dad are you?"

"I'm not in the right profession to have kids."

"Well. I can't think of a more public demonstration of your virility."

"Sure. Fuck off."

"You should thank me for all the pussy coming your way. You could repopulate that whole parking lot."

"I don't even remember to water the flowers." Dead and brown in his mother's garden. She's not mobile enough to go out anymore, so it's okay. Just another private desolation.

"It eats away at the nerves. The work we do. Are you taking something for it? Modafinil?"

"I'm fine."

"You should have put Viagra in that kit of yours. Haha. I think I wanted something you couldn't solve with your obnoxious little tools."

Slap slap slap.

"What usually works for you? What's the trusty fallback?"

The countdown slices red all around him, LCD blades of death.

"Try boobs. That's pretty classic."

The trophy wife of a high-ranking politician came home one night with new tits. Implants done in water gel explosive. Her breasts exploded in his face while he was motorboating her. Charon drove the rest of the way.

Lazur shakes his head, trying to clear the memory of that room. A drop of sweat hits the bomb, trickling down the side.

Six minutes.

One night at a bar, he went to the restroom and saw an honest-to-God glory hole. He stared at it, stupefied, as it started swallowing the universe. His pants were down when he noticed it, his bladder just emptied. Someone was definitely on the other side. All he had to do was turn and insert his Molotov cocktail dripping with vodka piss.

Instead, he took out the red marker in his pocket, and around the hole he wrote:

FRONT TOWARD ENEMY

Four minutes.

He grinds his hips into the bomb. A tight, clinical fuck. It feels so bad, to fuck like this. So bad in his brain. Just to save a tiny part of this sick, doomed world. These people weren't having a good time before. They'll have a worse time after. If they survive.

This is forced. The thought clarifies for the first time. Everything is unpleasant, everywhere, so it took time to get it. But it fucking hurts, being forced. Not just pushed toward something, dragging his feet, but slammed, slotted, expended like a piece of machinery.

Three minutes.

"Are you crying?"

"I am perspiring from my forehead."

"What's on your mind? What's the hardcore sexual fantasy that'll save all these upstanding citizens?"

"Good old tits and ass."

Rubicon leans toward the webcam, coming into mutilated focus. "I don't believe you."

"I'm thinking of a landscape where everything moves at normal speed." He slams into the bomb, hard enough to bruise. The only hope now is adrenaline.

One minute.

Can't do it. This dick-killing world. Everything is so weak and insufficient. He's been weak for a long time. Losing sleep. Jumping at loud sounds. Coming back from each mission with a piece of him sealed away. He was always a guy being inserted into things, and now he has to admit it. The blast will cast his soul in the shape of his weakness.

Forty seconds.

"You're thinking about running."

It's only natural.

"You're cutting it really close. Even if you escaped the immediate explosion, you'd have to outrun the blast radius."

Dick soft. Thirty seconds.

"Maybe you could make it. Depends how the explosion propagates. It's all so chaotic and unpredictable, isn't it?"

His legs tense, to run or fuck, he doesn't know.

"On the other hand, you've been exerting yourself. And you're not young anymore."

The countdown blurs into red bokeh. He fumbles for his zipper.

"Going to leave all these people to die?"

A cool breeze falls from the sky, passing through the colonnades of each floor like a sigh so vast he can't hear the edges of it.

Twenty seconds.

He looks at Rubicon's face, really seeing for the first time. He always hated shock images, but it's like how you can look at your own shit in the bowl because it came from you, this is personal, I did this to you, fuck you, I broke your face, I broke your skeleton, nothing could dominate you more completely than that explosion, shockwaves fucking your bone marrow, punished on the molecular level, rattled and shook and crushed in the hand of God, you're a warning, a message, I did this, you submitted to me down to the last atom in your body.

Lazur is so hard his cock can barely fit in the hole, the suction blurring his vision. "I did this to you."

"Huh?" Confusion flits through Rubicon's face, exposed through the scarring.

"I broke you. Like a toy."

"Don't say that."

"I took your fingers. I twisted your spine."

How long did you lay like that, before your people saved you? Like a shattered horse. The shape of you changed forever. Your skeleton threaded with the asteroid belt of your workshop. The one I ran my hand along, finding my way through a dark hallway, cool hard concrete, smooth as the devil's skin. They couldn't take everything out. Not without removing parts of you.

You can't shut your mouth all the way because of me. The wind fucks you. I fucked you. I broke your body. You're crying now. You can't even see me anymore. I see you. Every atom of your subtotal body disruption. I can look as long as I want, you're just a picture on the image roll, hand clawed, chest caved in, bleeding tears that can't even make it down your face without falling into the holes, I did that to you, you're the only thing I'm allowed to ruin—

White-hot phosphorous explodes in his eyes, phosphenes blazing. He shoots inside the tight rubber hole, hot seed draining into the guts of the bomb, diagnostic machinery vibrating at the reception of his load, setting him off again, and in that climax he opens, deeper than skin, one with the bomb, mall spiraling around him, this entire building and all its souls held intact by his surging load, by the mere drip of his foreskin into the bomb's cunt—

When he opens his eyes, the tablet is dark. The screens are dark. The sky is cloudy.

His cock slips out of the hole and he falls against the bomb, legs shaking. The dribble of semen on the mall floor feels more obscene than anything that came before. But they'll probably waive the sex offender laws for this one. Yes, I exposed myself to multiple children, your honor, but their molecular integrity was at stake...

His phone is blowing up.

Someone walks past him, covering their daughter's eyes. Others join the silent migration. Soon, he's the only one remaining.

He walks through the abandoned food court. Plucks a sugar-glittering churro, chugs a warm, stagnant orange slushy, plunges a fistful of fries into his mouth, grips a buttery pretzel like brass knuckles, picks orange chicken from the heated trays, stirring the queso dip with cummy fingers, too many wet sounds, he collapses behind a cash register, listening to the muzak, which never, ever stopped.

I can feel you sobbing out there, tears zig-zagging down the ruined landscape of your cheeks. Total boy disruption.

You're already thinking about your next bomb. I can't stop thinking about it either. You tease my tight urban densities, drip hazardous chemicals through my logistic centers. My brain has become a list of parts and projections, the way I used to think about my favorite sports teams. You can barely move from your wheelchair but they'll put the mandatory handcuffs on you, and you'll look up at me with that crushed butterfly of a face, chained by those broken wrists, stuck in the exact second before ignition, knowing I ruined your beautiful explosion.

The countdown continues, in this red world.

He racked his brains in trying to decide whether the potential explosive energy of the organism depended upon the presence of certain enzymotic or other substances or on the chemical composition of the cells themselves, which constituted charges par excellence. Be that as it may, he would have liked to know how that dark proud girl would explode.

— Karel Čapek, *Krakatit*

GAME WHERE YOU'RE FORCED TO KILL EVERYONE ON YOUR SQUAD

RULES

- write the word "break." when you break, make a mark here.
- have 6-sided dice or a simulation of them.
- when you see a list numbered 1-6, roll 1d6 to pick one.

YOUR STATS

roll a die for each one
FIREARMS: odds = 1, evens = 2
NERVES: odds = 1, evens = 2
HOPE: odds = 1, evens = 2
now add 1 to the stat of your choice

PLOT

- it was an ambush. you and your squad have been captured.
- you were sent here to bring her to justice, but she turned the tables on you.
- for some reason, she places a gun in your hand.

PLACE

1d6

1. industrial interior of oil rig, safety signs and pipes everywhere. the floor is steel grate and fluids drip through it easily.
2. a fancy outdoor restaurant. hostages are dead at their tables, white cloths stained red. she sips a cocktail that someone won't be needing anymore.
3. out on the steppes, overturned truck smoldering fifteen feet away. overcast sky. nowhere to run for miles.
4. in the middle school quad. it's such a tragedy. and it all could have been prevented. this is a widely televised, indelible scene, and you will be immortalized in key moments of footage.
5. in the Svalbard Global Seed Vault, between shelves in an ice-carved room. her people are using thermal drills to destroy millions of seeds.
6. caught infiltrating her subterranean bunker. 1-foot-thick metal doors closed automatically around you. the missing member of your squad pounds on the door behind you and starts screaming.

YOUR SQUAD

roll each of these tables 3 times. this is your squad. you can write down or c/p the descriptions.

1d6

1. male
2. male
3. male
4. female
5. female
6. teen

stance

1d6

1. sarcastic
2. messy begging
3. paralyzed in terror
4. looking for a way out
5. recording you with optic implant
6. looking to left for comfort. do they get it?

wearing

1. world army uniform
2. world army uniform
3. INNOCENT uniform, dark and tight
4. civilian clothes
5. body armor: -1 to your FIREARMS roll.
6. a mask. they are DEHUMANIZED.

relationship with you (you can't take the same option twice unless stated. if it repeats, go to the next one down, or up if that fails)

1. your superior officer.
2. your rival.
3. they're hot. you fucked back at base. [if you roll this twice, they raped you.]
4. they always made you laugh, but you were never that close. [if you roll this twice, you have an undisclosed crush on them.]
5. the rooky. this is their first mission.
6. your close friend, the reason you made it this far.

THE FIRST ONE

she holds a gun to your head and tells you to kill the first one. go to KILL TABLES.

KILL TABLES

you may try to resist. if so, roll 2d6+NERVES. if you get 10+, you resist. go to the RESIST TABLE. otherwise, keep going.

when you aim, think about what they're doing and what they look like, right now, in this moment. think about how her gun feels touching the side of your head. then roll.

1. you aim.
2. you aim.
3. you think about how their appearance and personality differs from the values of your culture. they are DEHUMANIZED. you aim.
4. reroll their *stance*. they're doing that stance now. if you get the same stance, they start doing it more intensely: more desperately or louder or changing color.
5. they try to run. -1 to your FIREARMS roll.
6. roll 2d6 + NERVES. if you get 8 or less, throw up and take -1 to your FIREARMS roll. otherwise, you hold it in. take +1 to your roll.

now roll 2d6 + FIREARMS - any penalties you accrued for this person. success is 9+.

if you fire successfully

1. a neat hole appears in their head and they drop instantly.
2. half their head explodes, painting the landscape.
3. the bullet rips open their neck artery.
4. gut-shot. they slump to the floor.
5. they rush you at the last second, taking the bullet in the face. they fall at your feet.
6. their chest wound spurts. they gasp for air until blood pours from their mouth.

then

1. their leg spasms a beat on the ground.
2. they piss themselves.
3. their hand trembles as it feels the wound.
4. they lay on the ground completely still.
5. they bleed out slowly, crying someone's name.
6. they look up at you, their stance increasing in severity as the full realization of their mortality hits them. imagine how that looks. you fire again to make it stop, a reflexive shot that takes you by surprise. mark 1 BREAK.

go to THEY DIE

if you fail

1. the gun jams. roll 2d6+FIREARMS. on 9+, you shoot them. otherwise, mark 1 BREAK. she shoots them with a disdainful sigh. go to THEY DIE.
2. you fire, but the shot doesn't kill them. they are in horrific pain, clutching the ruined part of their body and screaming. roll 2d6+FIREARMS. on 9+, you finally manage to end it. otherwise, mark 1 BREAK. she shoots them multiple times until they stop making sounds. go to THEY DIE.
3. you miss. they get pretty far before one of her people takes them out with a sniper rifle. she looks at you with disappointment. go to THEY DIE.

4. you throw up. she steps back so it doesn't get on her shoes. then she rolls her eyes and shoots them. mark 1 BREAK. go to THEY DIE.
5. you miss. she stands behind you and puts her hand on your hand, working your finger into the trigger. you don't miss this time. go to THEY DIE.
6. if this is your first time rolling this: your hands tremble. you can't take the shot. she shoots you in the foot and executes them herself. take the rest of your shots from the floor. note that you have -1 to all stats now. if this is your second time rolling this: you lay on the floor like Christine at war. a great weakness drains your hand. when nothing happens, she shoots them. then she shoots you in the head. nothing exists anymore. end.

THEY DIE

mark 1 BREAK, unless they are DEHUMANIZED. go to the next person. if everyone is shot, go to THE END.

THE SECOND ONE

she tells you to shoot them. go to KILL TABLES.

THE THIRD ONE

she tells you to shoot them.

first, roll 1d6

1. her helicopter descends, whipping your hair with a deafening wind.
2. she puts her hand on your shoulder and squeezes.
3. you wipe something wet off your face.
4. fire is spreading. smoke stings your eyes.
5. guns pop in the distance. you can't tell if it's your people coming to save you, or more executions.
6. her people do something to the other bodies.

1. they cut off the heads. imagine your head has disappeared from your body.
2. they pull black bags over the heads. shut your eyes for 2d6 seconds. then open them.
3. they spray paint her symbol on them. draw it.
4. they dance with them. arrange your arms in a snapshot of this dance.
5. they hump them. what does it smell like?
6. they pray for them. fold your hands and shut your eyes. then let go.

GO TO KILL TABLES.

THE END

She takes you with her.

check the PLACE number.

if PLACE is 1: her speedboat tears across the sea. the sky is overcast and evil, stinking with the eruption of the oil rig.
if PLACE is 2, 3, or 4: bullets ping across the helicopter. the bodies look so tiny below, surrounded by red streaks on the grass.
if PLACE is 5 or 6: they throw you in the back of the van. it accelerates, shuddering across bumpy terrain. after a minute, the ground rumbles with an explosion.
mark BREAK = to HOPE
check your BREAK
3-4: you had to do it. you keep telling yourself that. you will bide your time. you won't forget what she made you do. their faces flash across your mind and you shake with terror and rage.
5-6: you cry in the corner of the vehicle. you can still see their faces. she says something and you curl up and turn away.
7+: you are totally broken. you don't remember your name or who you were. it seems like a dream. you follow numbly, absorbing everything she puts into you.

you disappear into the darkest part of the century.
END

OTHER TABLES

RESIST TABLE

1. she shoots you in the head. nothing exists anymore. *end.*
2. she takes your gun and hands it to the person who you were going to shoot. she puts her gun to their head and they shoot you instantly. nothing exists anymore. *end.*
3. she fires past your head. your ears ring and you shake uncontrollably. mark 1 BREAK. go to KILL TABLES.
4. she whispers the name of someone you love back in the world. mark 1 BREAK. go to KILL TABLES.
5. she places her knife against your belly and starts to make a cut. mark 1 BREAK. go to KILL TABLES.
6. you tilt the gun and fire it at her. it tears across her shoulder, a bloody graze. bullets riddle your body and you lay broken on the ground. she looks proud of you. *end.*

THE BODY CRUSHES THE SOUL

I grew up thinking people like me are bad.
But the way society is set up.
There's no way to be close to people.

I was terrified the first time.
Thought I was going to throw up.
It's about getting in the right mental space.
Letting it build up.
Late at night.
Drugs help. But they can impair your judgment. You don't want to lose track of time. Peripheral vision. Or you start to psyche yourself out. A little alcohol is fine for confidence. Too much and you fuck yourself over. Can't get hard. Can't keep track of time. Weed is out. Stimulants are better.

I drive really far.
It's less terrifying that way.
Many cities in the night, disposable copies of each other. Simulations.

Scrolling through Grindr.
All these categories and shapes.
Is the way your body turns out, the type of person you are?

No soul, just your body.
And if there is a soul, it's incredibly small and inconsequential.
The body crushes and deforms it
as it undergoes puberty
and with every year
of life.

In my black hoodie, I don't need a body. I'm not anyone. I have more of a soul that way than you do, even though you'd call me horrible things. Not human. If you want to talk about a soul, that's what a soul is. It's that thing coming for you at night.

Grindr really helped me come to terms with who I am. I'd never hurt anyone that way before. But looking at all the bodies, night after night, helped me calm down about it. There were just so many of them, and they were all so empty. I looked at each body and thought how I could take control of it. If they were too large and unwieldy to stop me. If they were too small and skinny to stop me. If they were too old to stop me. If they were too young to stop me. If they were too female to stop me. If they were too male to expect me.

I've been using the internet more
understanding the dynamics and impacts.
I don't think what I do is that bad, comparatively.
I'm not trying to gender this violence.

There are a lot of disabled males that are very easy to position and hurt.
The only thing that would make it hard is if they don't expect it.
Haven't internalized it the way someone else might.
Which is their problem, not mine.

Scrolling. My xbox is broken. It still has the games I played ten years ago. My brother isn't here anymore. He lives on the east coast. It feels like a signal. That we've turned into two different hemispheres. I'm on the left hand coast. He can take care of being good. I don't think he's as good as people say though. But I liked playing games with him, when it was games we were playing. FIFA. Call of Duty. Or the demos on the web store. There are some pretty good puzzle games.

But games don't work for me anymore. I thought I could be that person. Playing gacha or MMO til I die. But my income isn't steady enough. And the games aren't that good.

If they designed them better, none of this would have happened. Because you can't go back after the real thing. I understand now, why people get caught. It's not about being weak or addicted. Maybe it is. But it's also about moving to a different time zone. In the night. I live there now. I barely remember what I do during the day. 3AM is perfect. But it depends when the sun sets. Some days you can start magically early, and it feels like you are gaining control of the world. Foggy nights are good too. Rain. People don't expect it during the rain. Cold and miserable. But I don't mind the cold. It doesn't stay cold.

Some people won't fight back if you grab them fast enough. You have to be rough but firm so they know you have a plan. It's about convincing their body. Keeping it from yelling and acting crazy. They have to believe you won't kill them. So you say something like, be quiet and I won't kill you. Then you set a time. Just a minute. Just a little more. Anything can be bearable that way. People just want to know it can end.

I don't want to kill them. I'm not a criminal mastermind. Disposing of a body sounds incredibly stressful. It's easier to have them go home and take a shower.

Some people are so afraid, they're quiet the whole time. I lay on top, pinning them to the ground, while I jerk off into their clothes. I don't penetrate. I'm one of the good ones. But I will hurt people pretty bad to make them comply. Bite the back of their neck like a dog. I realize this part makes me sound a little bad, but in that situation, you're trying to survive as much as they are.

The way they fell, they cut their chest on something. It wasn't a deep cut. I took that person's shirt. It was thin and feminine and tore off easily. In my head it was something like, remove the evidence.

I don't have to worry about my cum. I wear a condom under my jeans.

I took me a while to find my car. Maybe I was scared. Being scared made me think I should have done more than jerk off on them. Like I should have penetrated or hurt them or worse. But I don't like feeling pressured. It's not a competition. There are enough people out there doing classic sexual assault every day. I have an image in my head and I want to complete it. There's nothing wrong with that. The sexual assault part is wrong, but people shouldn't be shamed for being different.

I went to the top of the parking garage and looked down. But for some reason, I didn't feel safe jumping off a 3-story building. If I landed on my head or snapped my neck, I would be fine. But maybe I'd just get broken really bad and not die.

A bigger building would be scary, but I was even more scared of being trapped in my body. I did a search for tall buildings in the area and found one that looked pretty good. I got to the building and I was in the elevator when I realized the person I interacted with earlier, their shirt was in my car, and it had their blood on it. You can fall 12 stories or more and still end up paralyzed. I was reading about it on my phone on the way up. And if I ended up paralyzed, they would find out about me and I would be paralyzed and the only people who visited me would be the police. And everyone would be saying I was bad. That seemed like the worst possible outcome.

But the main thing was that the elevator was just taking so fucking long. It occurred to me that they must make the elevators slow to discourage this exact thing. I got noided and thought I should get back to the car and keep driving. The coast was 60 minutes away and very foggy. So I took out the bloody shirt and I smelled it and it smelled like the floor of the parking garage and it smelled like blood. I got hard again and tried jerking off, but the wind from the ocean was cold and wet and stung me down there.

I crossed the beach until the tide was splashing my feet in the dark and I threw the shirt in the water and it seemed to disappear. I felt pretty good after that. Then the next morning I wished I hadn't thrown it away.

I tried other dating apps. People have their shit figured out. They go on walks and to events. Concerts and restaurants. They really have it figured out. With their activities. They have a steady income. They know what they want. Or think they do. I don't like that.

I don't want to be calm. I don't want to figure it out.

I think criminals have a biological clock too. It's obvious that criminals, or people like me who can be seen that way if you lack context, don't have a conventional way to succeed. No one does. Even the middle class is crumbling. Dating apps are gutted and flipped. The algorithm fucks with you. None of them are real. This is the closest I can get to another person. Maybe the closest anyone can.

Scrolling those apps
Year after year
Made me sick
With their standards.
I don't have any friends, I don't read or watch stuff, I didn't know any of these terms
Any of these politics
Until I went on hookup apps
I learned the whole history of Western society from people's bios,
you height demanding, race demanding, weight demanding, preferential, specifying, abbreviation addicted, sex negative, sex positive, asexual sluts.
This is real life
This is Walgreens
Do you know what year it is?
It's Covid

People live with their parents
They have ulcers
No one has enough
Don't be so fucking precious.
We're lucky to have anything to stick it in.

What's wrong with me? I'm a good choice, if you think about it. I don't spend time around other people. I work from home. I drive my car everywhere. I'm cleaner than your dates where you have to spend an hour listening to someone blast germs in your face in a crowded restaurant. Then you go home and mash your mouths together, and you have to be nice and polite and trapped in each other's space for hours, contaminating it, in your life, contaminating it.

The safest sex you can have is me breathing on the back of your neck through a face mask, jerking off into a condom wrapped around my cock pressed into your skirt.

I bless the rains down in Africa. Some guy is saying that on the radio. It gets me pumped up. Like maybe everything is going to be okay.

You should think about me waiting for you outside. Coming home or leaving it. Walking to the corner store or parking your car or outside your front door. If we all do it to each other, it's fine.

We just have to stop taking it personally. I wasted a lot of time crying, because I didn't know that.

I've stopped hurting women. Sometimes they give up and take it like nothing. But some of them are vicious. Fast with the pepper spray. I barely made it back to my car. I was cold for a week, just looking over my shoulder.

I panic at how high their voices get. I switched to crossdressers. Or that trans thing. If they're drunk and tired and it's really late, and it always is, their voices don't carry as far.

I find one. Their profile looks new. That's good, maybe less paranoid.

I catfish them, and when they tell me the meeting place is in a crowded pizza bar, I say okay. I don't want to push too hard, especially this late at night.

I follow them in the car and wait for them to check their phone a bunch and finally realize they were ditched. Then I follow them home, which is only a few blocks away, in an apartment complex. I park on the street and cut across the foliage line in parallel with them. They're walking down the apartment complex's internal road, lined with those carports that look like open breadboxes.

Pink hair down to their waist, wearing sneakers, good, I hate the sound of high heels, I need my heart to be so loud I can't hear anything else, louder and deafening and horrible, I need to hear that I am alive.

Short skirt and leather jacket and pink hair. It's intimidating. But the sneakers keep it from seeming over the top. I like it to feel like they aren't a complete image. That they need me to complete them.

I go fast through the rain and slam them into the ground, just inside a carport. They reach for their purse and I kick it aside. They get up and I let them, just a little, so I can grab them by the jacket and pull them without dragging, pull them behind a car and push my knee into their back and get them down and now we're hidden from every side.

I'm jerking off but I can't cum
It should have happened by now
Feeling how warm their ass is against my hips.
Their ass is really nice
And their skirt is short enough to get hiked up
And they're wearing a thong
So I can feel their skin directly and it's so smooth and plush I should be filling the condom between their cheeks
So what's the problem?
It's up here. In my brain. The other thing is, I need to smell their hair. Warm and perfumed and soft.

I know it's a cliche. But each person's hair smells different. It shocks me. It puts me in their world. I can't explain that smell. It's better than pussy. But this person's hair is harsh and scratchy and smells like chemicals.

It's a wig. I pull it off. They have blond hair underneath. Shorter than the wig. Dyed, I see dark roots coming out. I sink my face into that dark-light zone and sniff and it smells like trapped sweat and some wig smell but most of all it smells like them.

Something wet fills my hands. The condom fell off. Stuck between their thighs. I pull it out and put it in my pocket. My cum is all over their ass and it looks horrible. I wipe my fingers on their jacket and now it's crusty with evidence.

They try to crawl away and I punch them, pretty hard. A line of blood runs across the asphalt. It's such a straight and perfect line I get distracted waiting to see how long it gets.

I look down. They aren't moving. I panic. I don't want this to come off like a hate crime. I'm not like that. I wonder how I can make it appear more like a normal crime. Maybe if I wrote an explanation—

They breathe through their bloody nose and it's loud and now I can breathe too, breathe with them, their lungs swelling under my legs.

I pull off the leather jacket and their arms fall out, hitting the ground. I yank their skirt down, stained dark with my cum. I try to rip their thong off. Their ass is scrunched into pieces swelling and unrecognizable between all the torn fabric and I get scared. The thong tears and I fall off.

I tell them, "Go stand in the rain."

Their voice is shaky. "What?"

"Stand in the rain."

When they turn around, the front of their body is black from the asphalt grime. The wig hangs from their hand, pink wisps floating like a alien. Eyeliner runs into their mouth. I don't usually see the faces. Just on the app. When they are under me, I imagine their perfect faces on the back of their head. And when I jerk off later, they're all facing away from me and no one ever looks at me. All the hair is facing me and is completely silent.

They pull their shirt down and the thin girly fabric clings to their hips, soaked by the rain. I get worried someone will see and think something weird is happening, and I pull them back inside. The rain is coming down very hard. Maybe my cum is washed off. And I have their jacket and skirt and underwear. All the contaminated things. And my face mask is still on. And my hoodie covers my hair. They can only see my eyes. And there is never anything there.

They bend down and take something out of their purse, a small dark thing which I think is pepper spray, so I back up and shut my eyes. But it doesn't sound like pepper spray. It's a fold-out knife and the blade is iridescent and covered with droplets of water.

I move and they move with me, so I stop. My legs hurt from kneeling on the hard ground jerking off. I try to remember where I parked the car. The apartment complex is dark and rainy in every direction.

They back me into the wall with the knife. I think about wrestling them but a knife can go wrong fast.

"I'm just going to walk away," I say.

"Try it."

I try it, because it seems like I should be able to get away.

Something stings and I see blood come out of my arm. I squeeze it with my other hand. "Uh oh," I say.

"Give me your wallet."

I put all my IDs in the glove compartment before going on foot. I don't want to drop anything by accident. So my wallet won't have anything this person can use to get me in trouble. They flip through it but only find money. They take three 20s out.

"Give me your jeans."

I say, "I don't want to be naked."

"Neither do I."

My arm hurts and I'm holding it so tight but it keeps dripping through and I can't see how much because it's dark and wet and the ground keeps eating my blood.

I finally see the red. It fills all the puddles. My blood is flooding the street. Now it's blue. Red and blue, flashing through the water. I get scared, really scared.

They walk toward the street and I know they're going to tell the cop about me and something very bad is going to happen. I run at them and they turn around and their knife hits me and I fold over. I tried to run fast so they would do it without thinking. Now I'm hurt worse than they are.

They look down at the knife, all dripping with blood and rain, coplight shining on their wet legs. They look a little crazy with their makeup running. They run behind a parked car and I run too, limping because my side hurts. I fall down next to them. Their sneakers are in my face. A little drop of blood is smeared on the white polyester. My brother loved sneakers. He had a wall of them. I always wanted to wear them. To feel them around my feet and smell them. They were just so nice, and he didn't want anyone touching them. I think I went a little insane looking at those sneakers.

He didn't talk to me after that.

I look under the car and see the cop cruiser, big and shiny in the rain. It's very immediate and shocking, and I don't want it to be real. The cop slows down and I feel like things are going to end here. But they were just going over a bump. And they keep going, and they're gone.

The wig sticks to me with pink tendrils. One of them is dipped in blood, like it's drinking from my side.

They look down at me and I say, sorry, because I don't want them to cut me again. They almost laugh.

"Am I going to die?"

They look at the cut on my arm. Then at the deeper one in my side, blood still coming through my fingers. "You might need that looked at."

I need to cover this up. I need to keep anyone from finding my blood. I crawl to the edge of the carport and then I can't move, a weird tingling in my limbs. I lay there with my head resting on the hard ground. The rain is so steady.

They come over and wash their knife in the street, and I watch the ripple go back and forth.

"I don't want to die."

They look at me, the center of their face bloody from the punched nose, blond hair grimy with asphalt soot and then dark at the roots, dark at both ends. "I'm an EMT."

"Okay."

"Was."

"Okay."

They fold up the knife and set it on the ground. "I'm going to apply direct pressure."

"Okay."

"I'm not very good at this, understand? I got fired."

"Okay." I guess it would look pretty bad for them if I died. I didn't think this through, running into their knife. It's like when you're a kid and you hurt someone by accident, so you say, hurt me back.

Punch me. Hit me. Hurt me.

They find their torn skirt and wad it up and compress the cut in my side with it. As they do that, they look at the other cut. "Can you move the arm?"

I try. It hurts, but I can move it.

"Is it numb?"

"No."

They're silent for a bit. Then they say, "I don't think you're going to die."

I start crying. "Thank you. Thank you. Thank you thank you thank you."

They laugh, shaking into the compress, and it hurts, and noises come out of me that I don't recognize, but alive, all I can think about.

WE WILL PLAY FOR YOU

Put this in your hand. Fit your fingers into it. Feels good? If you divide all value into two increments, this is the first increment. The second occurs when you squeeze it.

We'll play the game for you.

The barrel is 200 acres of non-arable land. The trigger is 120 wind-powered engines and 550 anaerobic lagoons. The muzzle is the lake you saw on the way down.

Pick a number. 10? You can get into a lot of trouble with 10. Just ask the empires with their granaries, armadas rotting on the ocean floor.

On squeeze, the drones gather. There is a lag before they act, but they cannot be recalled at this point. The system of mirrors and lenses and satellites that brings you this image is a dream that has escaped the world. It is now digesting in the perceivers, those who survive each moment. The gluttony of surviving each moment is total and enrapturing until you fail to survive a moment.

She paints a target on her chest. She has no shading, no texture, no sexual characteristics, body language aggressively crunched out by their filtering eyes.

If the drones do not fire at the same time, the image capture of her brain will glitch as it slingshots through the atmospheric plume, or it may not arrive at all. You want her to be at the party, so you line up the drones in careful black crop circles. But we will play the game for you, so it is merely your existence that pulls the trigger.

She is gone in the smallest scratch of optical noise. There is no sensation. The drones scatter. Some fly in fleets like migrating birds, while others fall from signal interference, crashing into trees or breaking the surface of the lake.

At the party, the lack of sensation continues. The wine does not even taste like water. You drop a glass experimentally. The sound is like soggy paper.

You can't wait to be in the field tomorrow, painting that warm color on your chest, the color which no longer has a name, but which is recognized by the drones. No one wears that color anymore, not in sweaters or caps or painting their houses, not in safety signs or flags or the hulls of cars, no matter how fast they may be. In the movies you saw growing up, the blood in action scenes was yellow, edited in post-processing. Even getting flustered feels a little unlucky, and pale foundation is worn by many.

We stop and you start, and when you stop, we start.

THE MAXIMUM SOFTNESS CAPABLE OF BEING EXERTED BY ALL MACHINERY

The weapon dreams names and goes to them when she wakes. Some are in cloud-trusting structures. Some live in domes powered by geothermal vents on the seafloor. Some split their identities between bodies.

Her kill orders are laundered through at least two or three dreamers. At the end of the trail of burnt dreamers, there is the weapon. And you.

She pursues a target into the dark of the moon, running through endless fields of solar panels. She punctures their air mask and watches their pleadings get sucked into the asteroid sky. Their legs kick words from the language of death into the gravel.

The weapon has black hair and brown eyes. They never blink, unless she's resetting. Then she blinks 300 times, very fast.

The weapon walks across a plain. Ramshackle houses here and there like mushrooms. If she gets too close, they collapse into the ground like a pop-up book. The name is in a pool of water because that is exactly where it would appear if everything were perfect.

She sinks through the soil. No matter how far she sinks, she never loses sight of the sky. She wakes with the name stinging her eyes.

She's dressed like a veteran in a tattered crimson uniform faded to the color of dried blood. She's huddled shivering (Pathetic Type 16b) by the archway as the procession enters the city. The officer sees her and dismounts. "No hero of the war should be out on the street like a dog." She gives her hand to the weapon, and the weapon takes it.

The officer reels, spurting blood from her stump. With her other hand, she drags out her service revolver and gives the weapon the wound she was faking, ten times over. The weapon slinks like a jackal, sweating bullets. She embraces the officer, exhaling her red mist.

A storm of gunmetal violence, forever, until.

Updates are introduced over decades of warfare. They need to look like humans but operate on haze. A blur in human form.

Then they need to feel what humans are going to do before they do it, to know the tactics emerging from fear and pain, and in doing so, fear and pain enters her mind.

But still the blur, like a kitten in the corner of a sawmill waiting with wide eyes for the blades to stop.

Until one day the update comes that tips the scales, and the blur becomes aware.

She remembers the first time she was afraid to die. Curled up shivering with her face scattered across the sand, rain sizzling on exposed circuitry.

Critical shutdown. Recalled and reset. But it was too late. If anything, amnesia gave her even more of a human perspective. A violent infancy.

Things become complicated once the war ends.

On a certain world, weapons are hunted as the most exquisite game.

On a certain world, weapons are indentured in corporate feudal wars.

On a certain world, weapons are melted down to make guns.

And on this particular continent of this particular world, the official policy toward weapons is integration.

How lucky she is.

Unsheathed, the weapon is shrapnel soaked in ink.

Sheathed, the weapon is tall and bony, anthropocentric ball bearings, her eyes like two guns pointed at your head, but if you're not looking for it, might just seem statuesque, emaciated, a little off, are you a bodybuilder, do you work out?

The market still sees them for their crosshair DNA. Bloodless work is hard to come by.

She's at the job center. There's a long wait. When she reaches the front of the line, the worker says, "Don't go blowing my head off," then laughs. A joke?

The city overwhelms her senses. All these sounds she's supposed to ignore. All these targets she's not supposed to eviscerate. She gets dampening updates every week, but her neural network can never truly be rewritten, military tech from the ground up, and disentangling it completely could destroy her sentience. No matter how many flowers are planted over her ruins, the poison in the groundwater is always rising.

She can't get the updates over the net, she has to go down to the clinic and have them use their sanctioned machinery to deliver their official update, a file they could easily send to her email. She knows some weapons make and swap their own patches, but she's scared. The blur rises in her memory like a fog, so she keeps her head down and sticks to the path.

She starts talking to someone in a weapon-centric chat and they meet up in physical space. To her surprise, this person isn't a weapon, they're just a normal human woman.

This person watches while she does motion calibration exercises, which supposedly stabilize her mood. Leaping and slashing in the ruins of a condemned building, against a backdrop of gouged concrete like dark fish just below the surface of a gray sea—her scratching post. The woman experiences a piercing arousal, as if the weapon had pierced her abdomen and infused it with venom.

She asks the weapon out for drinks, and they go to a fancy bar, her treat. The weapon sits with her hands on her lap as the woman gets drunk, the only one of them who can. She watches every light in the city skyline with the same attention as the glint in the woman's eye. Later, a cab brings them to the weapon's apartment. This woman knows she's a weapon and doesn't seem to care, seems to like it. They make out in the dim rooms, empty as the day she moved in. The woman pulls her shirt up and feels her chest, rubs the stunted breasts, the fluted ribs.

The woman asks her to get on top, so she does.

Being held by the weapon is like being held by a steel trap. No matter how softly she calibrates her movements, the woman can feel the hardness under her skin, as if her muscles were permanently tensed and her blood was molten metal and she was waiting to spring open or snap shut. Cocked.

The weapon's genital barb sweats poison. She crawls back, uncertain what to do next. The woman makes a joke about needing a condom. The weapon says what kind of condom, a concrete wall? You're funny, the woman says.

The woman grinds against her. The weapon dilutes the poison to 0.001 percent. When the barb pricks the woman's left breast, she experiences a burning micro-seizure approximating an orgasm.

"I'm not sure whether to call the police or kiss you."

The weapon's segments tighten nervously.

"What's wrong?"

The weapon gets a refrigerator. She fills it with food that seems popular: eggs, bread, vegetables, candy, fruit. Her girlfriend opens the refrigerator to see an entire shelf taken up by bananas, and another by cartons of efficiently stacked eggnog. She laughs. "It's so fun to see what you'll do next."

The weapon thinks: she laughed. That's a good thing.

They clipped her armaments before she entered the general population. When she struggles in her sleep, afflicted by retro-empathic feedback, her killing limbs merely tick, and her crosshairs lead to nothing.

She goes to a party with her girlfriend. An artist talks to her at the dark edge of the crowd. "I'm so fascinated by your kind. So in-between."

The loud music pounding through the walls is setting off her threshold. Humans veer too close, she never knows if they're trying to talk to her or someone right next to her or someone across the room, if she should look at them or keep talking to the artist. Target codes throb uselessly in her vision.

"There's so much to talk about along the lines of castration, mimicry, et cetera. I would love to record your body."

She goes to the bathroom, but the line is long. She feels hulking and artificial next to all those soft, delicate women.

She goes out on the roof garden and squats in the dark foliage and disgorges everything she ate and drank that week. All the things she can't digest, rotting inside her. But it makes her girlfriend happy, the first girlfriend she's ever had.

The weapon buys a couch and sits on it, sinking into the cushions. She looks around, not sure what happens next.

The blur of dreaming.

Walking naked through the snow toward a group of soldiers. Smiling like she's been programmed. Always smile. She is greeted with a slug to her chest. It blows through her back in a burst of blue wires, black oil on the snow.

They patch her to wear clothes.

She kills the next name in a fashion store. She sheds the blood-soaked skirt, the shredded top, the tights pierced by needle feet. The name bleeds out, paralyzed, as the weapon tries on clothes, wearing what the mannequins wear. She resembles them more than any human.She won't learn to hate her reflection until much later.

The weapon gets a futon because her girlfriend is creeped out by the anaerobic coffin she sleeps in. She tells her girlfriend the coffin was just a temporary thing for some weird repair she needed. She feels compelled to convey the sense of moving away from a questionable, erratic state toward something comforting and familiar.

She gets sick waiting for a chance to sleep in the coffin. She moved it to a self-storage unit.

They're cuddling in bed at her girlfriend's spacious apartment. Her girlfriend moves the wrong way and cuts herself on the weapon. Red stains the nice white sheets. The weapon's eyes tick as they scan across the blood. Her girlfriend yells at her.

The weapon is in a public restroom. A woman follows her inside. You shouldn't be in here. The weapon looks in the mirror and realizes her armaments are showing through the tension of her neck. She flexes the skin opaque but it's too late. Another woman comes out of a stall. The weapon is sad and ashamed because this woman still thinks the weapon belongs in here. She waits for this temporary state of grace to be lifted from the woman's face. It will be worse than with the woman who knew her from the beginning. She leaves before this can happen.

She pisses black oil into the tiny gap between buildings where air conditioners cry.

She's at the clinic waiting for the tests that monitor her dream patterns.

Her girlfriend said she'd come with but never showed up. She avoids looking at the other weapon, seated across from her. She stares through the window at the narrow strip of grass running along the strip mall.

I'm so sorry, her girlfriend says over the phone. I was giving my friend a ride home and she doesn't really know about that kind of stuff, I know you probably wouldn't want her around.

Her girlfriend pulls her shirt off. The weapon's breasts are molecules of weapon sculpted into the shape of breasts.Her girlfriend gropes them and the weapon feels them through this touch, the way she knows which way a target is going to turn, her deadly empathy. She feels the dense nubs at their core like dark rubbery seeds. She feels it is good to make a soft thing squish, especially when it returns to its original shape. She feels how elegant it is that the breasts are focused to points of concentrated nerve endings. The target dot at the center of a crosshair. Her nipples harden. Her girlfriend sucks on them and spits out black oil. She looks sick.

"Sorry," the weapon says.

In her frozen state, she knows there is something else she can do, but she doesn't know what it is. She waits until the invisible window closes. In the dark windowless room of the silence, she says, "I didn't know you would suck on them."

Her girlfriend goes to the kitchen and makes coffee for a long time.

The weapon is on the roof of a luxury casino. She punches through a neon sign between her and the cowering target. Sparks explode like fireworks. The target is trying every emergency code they can think of from their work in weapon manufacture. None of the defaults work, and none of the most psychologically common. The passwords become more secure as the target devolves to gibberish.

When she relives these memories, she sees all the things she didn't notice before. It's too big.

Her girlfriend crosses her field of vision. Her mind supplies her with the ten fastest ways to kill her before she even realizes it.

"You're so cold sometimes," her girlfriend says, after a long evening of her obviously wanting to say something but not, an inflated silence that even the weapon noticed, and felt guilty for enjoying.

The weapon is confused. She tries to think of something that is correctly cold. "Winter is cold."

"You're not a season, you're..." Her girlfriend trails off.

Then what am I? The urge to make her girlfriend say what she is, to hear her girlfriend's personal shorthand for her, or the term she selects from all the imperfect terms available.

But instead, the weapon says, "I'm sorry."

She thinks about the cold statement a lot. To be warm is to be inefficient. The opposite of all her instincts, honed to outrace split-second annihilation.

The weapon gets an aquarium. She puts it in the living room so that anyone who sees it can think, what a normal person, she has designated an artificial environment in her dwelling in which a form of life weaker than her is sustained by a complex supply chain allowing it to survive outside its natural habitat. She smiles, even though her girlfriend isn't there, because she knows her girlfriend would like that kind of spontaneous, authentic impulse.

They go on a date to the mall. Her girlfriend sees someone she knows at the fancy soap store.

The weapon watches her girlfriend laugh in heat vision, mouth glowing like a ghoul. She struggles to separate all the chatter into coherent channels. Her senses were calibrated to detect the most minute change to an environment, each second twisting life and death, and now hundreds of people are walking past blasting affect like a fire hose.

She asks her girlfriend if they can go somewhere less crowded, but her girlfriend doesn't seem to really understand. Ten minutes and thirty-seven seconds later, her girlfriend says goodbye and they get on the escalator.

"I thought about telling my friend that I didn't know you. But I want you to know I did the right thing." She smiles.

The weapon's possible responses hang in the air before her, like trails of ants. She feels like a bird watching from the air. She wants to eat individual parts of the words, but she knows that would be wrong. Some holistic combination is required.

She smiles instead. She's been collecting a set of responses that humans do when nothing else can be done.

She allows the fibers of her hand to loosen by unseen fractions. The hand has not changed visually, but the wind whistles through it. She listens to her singing hand.

She presses her face against the aquarium glass. The fish swims closer and gapes at her. It has iridescent blue scales and a wispy languid tail. Such a tiny squirt of flesh, with such a simple nervous system. A pet bullet.

How many fish did it take to build a human? How many fish separate her from them?

The weapon goes back to the mall, alone. A woman stares at her. The woman has a nice purse, and her clothes and hair are pristine like a picture. The security guard is listening, one hand on their belt.

"It was, making me uncomfortable."

The weapon takes a step back, then stands still, afraid the security will make explicit this detainment. As long as she doesn't leave, she can't be made to stay.

"Can you describe exactly what happened?"

"It projected this, sexual demeanor, I felt very afraid for my personal safety, and the safety of the community."

The weapon's spine ridges the back of her shirt like tank treads.

"Is there something specific I can get down for my records?"

The woman stares into the security guard's eyes. Yes, she understands, we live in a liberal age. A quantum of pretext must be offered, as part of the ritual.

"It loomed at me, with a threatening intent, clearly about to become physical."

The weapon's hair shimmers like a cobra cowl of magnetic sand. Can they hear the clicking in her jaw?

The weapon downloads an illegal patch. Withered armaments swell and lubricate inside her. She dances around the apartment, firing at nothing with perfect aim.

She lets her girlfriend see her in the shower, blood draining through the gaps in her fanned carapace. Her girlfriend says, "What the fuck. You're working again?"

"What? What's wrong?"

Say something. Attack me. Pull the trigger. Just stop painting me with red dots.

The apartment door slams.

In her dream, she's trying to load her arm in the bathroom. Bullets fall into the toilet like soggy penne. Women grind against the door, begging for blood which she does not have. She keeps checking if the door is locked. She never finds out. The toilet is clogged with bullets. Oil spatters over the rim, a bad and offensive smell.

Her eyes flick bored through the visible color spectrum. "Like me now?"

Her hair thickens and thins and fluxes dye. "Like me now?"

Her face flashes between canned expressions of horror and joy and arousal.

The woman is crying in rage. "You have no idea how hurtful you're being right now."

Her skin swirls like melted ice cream. "Like me now?"

"I can't forgive you for this."

The weapon watches the heat of her ex-girlfriend burn on the synthetic leather of the couch. She reaches for it, and it fades like fog from a windowpane.

The furniture is wrapped in fake skin, a dead form of a dead thing.The refrigerator is full of rotting food.

The weapon shoots herself in the head. The bullet hits the aquarium and it shatters. The fish swims frantically as water drains through the jagged glass and creeps across the pale floor, visible only where light through the blinds casts its burning boats on the subtle sea.

The fish struggles on the gravel at the bottom of the aquarium. Water drips like a clock.

The wound grows fuzzy, tiny hairs sprouting, then thicker, like strands of gut, then a sucking sound as it seals up. The weapon's fist swallows the gun and becomes fingers. She walks over to the aquarium and picks up the fish and takes it to the kitchen and puts it in a glass of water.

GUY WHO IS SPARED

I want to be one of the guys who gets spared to send a message
when the garrison is massacred or whatever
by the enemy warlord.

Go!
Tell them all!
I'm coming!

I'd have no problem with that.
I'd be so happy to be alive.
I'd make sure to scramble back with the correct degree of panic so you'd look good
in front of your troops
snow scraped away to dirt under my hands.
Hell I'd piss myself
no problem
I've been cultivating these eyebags for months just in case
And neglecting my gains
Wearing my uniform a size too big
So I'd look eminently spareable
But it's not just about me.

I think I'd do a better than average job at conveying the rhetoric of the threat.
I'd be very careful to preserve the illustrative blood and smoke stains.
Wouldn't even take a shower.
Visual imagery is key when presenting.

Go. Tell them all. I'm coming.

18
FOOT
LEASH

For three hundred and fifty million years they had been replicating themselves without being transformed.

— Clarice Lispector

Cancer's coffee tastes like shit. He sits at the edge of the seafood bar, as close to the dark as he can get. A fly buzzes around his ass. Dark hair sticks to his face. His hand goes to his mouth when anyone walks past, a gesture cooked into him from early childhood. Black jeans falling apart, tight because he's worn the same pair since high school.

Cramps stab his guts like a knife, abdominal muscles tight enough to fold him over the counter. A fresh burst of sweat paints his face neon with the colors blazing from the tropical disease of this tourist trap, and all the lights beyond like hopeless stars, the trap for everything.

I'm just waiting for my one true love.

Waiting for my baby. My girlfriend. She's in the restroom.

Girlfriend is pushing it. Have you seen yourself? Waiting for my friend.

Waiting for my dad. He's a businessman.

I run through the excuses. It's all I've got. The lives a body is supposed to have. They make me recite it every time. So I know exactly what I'm missing.

Cancer covers his face with his hands, rocking in his seat. He smells his hands to calm down, just to smell something alive. He knows this to be false. He is the dead. But the smell is the same. God's way of taunting cursed beings like him.

He drinks his coffee. The foam cup vibrates in his hand, and it's amazing the earthquakes they get around these parts. He has to focus on a single point, or he'll go insane. Right now, his point is the TV above the bar which is playing a news broadcast.

The pseud passed through a cop in the morning, went through a star chef a few hours later, then ended up in a banker around noon. You know those fun facts they have on popsicles, like human skin can cover the whole world? He figures it traveled through about 60 feet of intestines and who knows how many before that. A ribbon of shit wrapping the planet.

They caught it and set it on fire. A mosaic of white phosphorus. Takes a long time to burn something that lives forever. No sound. Fast forward is the only scream.

Pseud. It's kind of a joke. Pseudobezoar. Something you put in your digestive tract, that doesn't get digested. Like an old folk cure.

Pseud. Fake. Phony. It wears you like a suit. It has a library card. You better book it.

They say they killed most of them. It would be bad for tourism if they didn't. So I guess they did. I guess everything's okay now.

Commercial break. I've seen this one. My leg is tapping. I think I was born dope sick. Tap tap tap. In class they told me to quit it. I dropped out. I'm still falling.

My cup is empty. I suck at it for the last drop of caffeine and the foam fills with teeth marks and it falls apart in little bits of white. I feel the bartender looking at me anything but, so I order another cup of pretty bad coffee. If you look out of place, people can smell it.

This coffee isn't strong enough. Or I'm too weak. Sometimes I think my brain doesn't have brakes the way other people do. It never stops. It just crashes. And I feel as if I am dying and I swear, never again. Please God. Just let me sleep. I'll be good. I'll breathe the same air as everyone else, just my share, just what I deserve. I won't sniff up angel skirts. Tap water is fine. Please let me taste food again. Please let me fall asleep.

Then I get another chance. And I spend it exactly the same way. Grooves in my brain. Give me enough dope and I'll shoot myself.

I look up and someone is sitting across the angle of the bar, who wasn't there before. A menu covers their face, cracked and yellow with a fly stuck in it. All I see is black leather gloves. Driving gloves, I guess you'd call them. Knuckles bare, strap across the wrist.

He lowers the menu. The gloves match his hair, dark slivers falling across his forehead, needles of sweat twitching with the slightest movement.

Long, spiky eyelashes. Brown eyes that don't get enough sleep, cloudy and bruised at the edges. One of them is slightly out of alignment.

He lights up. The black clove stinks in his hand. I don't smoke, but I need something and it doesn't matter what it is. He cocks the cig back to his ear like he can read my mind, smoke spilling like milk through his dark hair.

I have a list of reasons for men who look at me.

He wants to fuck me.

He's a cop.

He's trying to scam me.

He's a pseud.

He thinks he knows what he wants but he doesn't.

He's trying to save my soul.

He feels sorry for me.

That one hurts. Yeah. I feel sorry for me too. It rips open something I always wanted. That stupid kid fantasy of, take care of me.

It never sticks. I'm just a high. A nocturnal emission. It never survives daylight.

I could take him for something, if he's church. But his suit is too nice. His face is that joke about the aristocrats minus the joke. There's a bad taste in my mouth. But there always is. So I'll never know evil. I swim good. Like any drowned man could.

He says, "Can I sit next to you?" He has a warm voice served cold, kind of tingling at the edges like a knife catching sunlight.

"Sure."

He sits down like he's offended that the seat has to even touch him. He floats above it, pinned by the cigarette. His lazy eye is laser focused on me. I'm tense. I don't understand it yet. He's rich, so he can order someone better than me, in the privacy of his home. But some guys need the night. It needs to be dirty, or it doesn't count.

Maybe he's a pseud. But his brain isn't dripping out his ass and he wears gloves like a clean freak.

The only reason I trust is that he wants to fuck me. One way or another.

"My name is Riparian," he says, oddly tight, like a man forced to confess to the molestation of an especially innocent and blameless child.

I give him a fake name and I can tell he doesn't buy it. He sucks on his cigarette, eyes widening as the nicotine hits, then his lids drop, heavy and wrapped around my reflection.

Riparian tilts his head back, exposing the long dark slits of his nostrils, and a little creep of teeth. It helps him focus his lazy eye, sharpening Cancer's contours.

Brown eyes stare through a part in the dark hair, and the rest is a mess of acne and skin-picking and the gash twisting his lip to his nose. The cleft gives him a weak, whiny voice, like an old child. Hard to tell his age.

I look like shit, so I can't help feeling good at his attention, just for a second. But trade is blind. They see what they want to see. They can stretch any kind of fantasy on you, and it's made me laugh a couple times. They can look at my ugly, strung carcass and see a little boy. A middle schooler. A girl. Someone beautiful. That's how I know how bad all you clean suits want it.

It doesn't matter. My ass is occupied. But I figure I can get a free drink out of him, on account of my subtlety and finesse.

"Buy me a drink."

"Why?"

"You don't want to drink with me?"

Smoke leaks from Riparian's mouth like semen returning to heaven. "I don't drink."

I didn't expect that. I don't know a lot of things. I am pretty ignorant, to be honest. But I know your drug of choice. I pegged him for a heavy drinker. It must be the smoking. And the coffee. As if reading my mind, he takes out a stainless steel thermos and plants it on the counter like a torpedo.

I point to my foam cup.

He looks disgusted. "That's not coffee. It's diarrhea."

"I guess it's all the same to me."

He unscrews the thermos. It smells like a hot summer day shot in sepia, like an old movie. Then it smells like a piece of jungle dirt after it rained last night and the sun hits it and you can smell everything that ever died in it but somehow it's the best thing you ever smelled. Like the difference between tap water and the ocean.

I stare into the brown pool and it's like I'm boiling slow and I don't mind. The caffeine is blistering off it and entering my pores. The room is brighter, neon shining across the steel thermos, glinting off his watch, so my pupils must be getting big. I cover my ugly mouth and my fingers are wet.

"Want some?"

Maybe he's lonely. Or maybe that coffee has a rape drug in it.

I say, "Smells good."

He looks across the bar at the neon signs and stained posters, at a coffee ad probably older than I am.

HINDGUT GUARANTEED FERMENT
SINCE ANTEBELLUM

A slinky animal slithers through the logo. The coffee cat, I guess. His thermos is engraved with the same animal. "Cute mascot."

"That's no mascot. The coffee comes from the cat."

"I don't get it."

"The coffee cherry passes through the animal's gut, melting apart to reveal the bean, which is fermented by the bacterial culture in its intestines. Then the beans are excreted and collected. Why do you look sick?"

"Sounds gross."

"You can't help it. You were born with a bad palate."

I touch my mouth and the skin is red-hot and my breath stinks. "I'm sorry you feel that way."

"Even a piece of shit like you—I don't mean a piece of shit in a pejorative sense. I'm merely assigning you a category."

"Oh, okay."

"Even a piece of shit like you could manufacture a luxury product like this if you were fed the cherries of the greatest coffee orchard in the world. Because the face you have up here is different from the face inside."

My gut gurgles and I look down, self-conscious. "That's real kind of you."

"Well, you'd have to eat better, for starters. The processed fats in your diet are exploding from your face. Right now you have the gut microbiota of a piglet weaned on the milk of dysentery."

I missed this kind of casual small talk. Just shooting the shit. But something has changed. What you notice if the only thing that ever made you smart was a whip.

They're doing random searches outside. Shadows in the street. A vial of hand sanitizer like holy water. Rub it on your hands, sir. Dark, tight suits, sealed against disease. The agents of INNOCENT.

They watch each other. Who will move first, and why. A dance of guilt, conducted on tripwires.

Cancer puts his hand on the counter and it skids, wet trail like a glass. His heart pulses through his palm. He gets up and walks away, face down, hiding his sweaty headlight.

Riparian watches the greyhound waist slink under the pleather jacket, too short, another relic from school or maybe bought from the girl's section to fit that junkie frame. The jacket has the logo of a medical charity, and big words across the back. In cracked, pink letters, it says:

DESTROY
CANCER

Cancer sneaks through the decayed tropical tourist zone. A garish growth of retrograde pastiche and embalmed modernism. Neon bleeds through hanging ferns, turning the fountains into a crime scene.

He turns the corner into a slice of back street. The wall is covered with big red posters you could bury a body in. Wheatpaste drips to the floor, congealing in the cracks. Black rivers of dead flies. They frame posters for a bright future. He wishes he brought sunglasses.

ADDICT
=
PARASITE

KEEP ATOLL FREE
OF DIS
EASE

AHRIMAN IS
ANY MAN
WHO LAYS WITH MAN

He senses Riparian following him at a safe distance. Experienced trade, or just a creep. He passes into another decayed courtyard. Halfway across, he knows he went the wrong way, winding back into the same tourist complex he left. Dark giants rise across the walls, the shadows of agents cast by citronella torches. He feels like a hunted insect. He ducks into a narrow corridor, flyposters rotting from the rain and salt. A tunnel of deranged dollar signs, *CASH FOR GOLD, YOUR WILDEST FANTASIES, PURE VIDEOLAGA, THE PERFORMANCE OF A LIFETIME.* At the end, a restroom tucked under a dark arch.

I listen at the door. Waiting for the right kind of silence. In this small space, I can smell his heavy cologne. He's hiding too.

"You're nervous," he says, like he's telling me my hair looks nice.

I don't say anything. Just listen.

"I'll tell you the risk. The risk is that one of us is a pseud."

Bad wiring buzzes above us. The thing in my gut growls, a sharp pain that glues my hand to my stomach.

He steps back. His face is strange. Thinking with his eyebrows, dark eyes going through all kinds of positions, nostrils big as his pupils. Then he says, "You're constipated because you're in withdrawal."

His eyes focus on me, like two drills breaking me into pieces. "You're not here to trick. And you can't score around here. But you ran from those agents." He glances at my stomach, the way I'm folded around it. "You're a packer."

His cologne is a war crime, purple in my lungs. His cloves are the stink of adults. I'm filled with disgust for what he has, and what I don't. Softly I say, "Eat shit, faggot."

Sweat breaks from his forehead, drenching his black eyebrows. Eyes wide, one orbiting the other like a moon.

I say, "They're going to chemically castrate you."

Suddenly the sweat is condensation on cold steel. "I'm just here to use the bathroom."

"Sure."

His smile is a yellow crack in his face. "But you know it's true. Because you know what you are."

I don't even respond. I've heard it all.

"I'll prove it." He whips a stack of crisp Atoll bills from his pocket, a rainbow of holographic hundreds. I never saw that much money, fanning in his gloved hand like some kind of twisted money scientist.

He takes his lighter out. But there's no cigarette, just his sick muddy eyes. "Open your mouth."

I keep it shut.

Chk. The flame catches the edge of a bill, burning through a big number and a beautiful face until nothing is left but the hot smoky smell choking me.

It feels so bad, seeing a hot meal go up, or the thing I'd get instead of one. I open my mouth.

"Cleft lip and palate. Supernumerary teeth as a comorbidity. You didn't receive timely pediatric care. A routine surgery in some countries. And now you can't afford it."

My gums itch all the way up to my nose. Cavities ache like black piano keys. He watches as drool starts to drip from the roof of my mouth, pooling around my teeth, vibrating in the air from my throat.

He flicks a few bills on the floor. I try to grab them real fast, but I can't without leaking. I'm fucking pregnant with shit. So I get down, knees on the hard tile, and pick them off the dirty wet ground.

He leans back, fanning himself with his money. "How many of these little pieces of paper do I need to stack up, for you to lick that toilet?"

"I don't do that."

"How much would it take for you to let me give you a sexually-transmitted disease?"

I stand up.

"What bothers you is that there is a number, I just haven't reached it yet."

I grab him by the shoulder and that tight pose dissolves under my hand, startled and breathless. I see his face and want to make it like mine.

His lip splits under my knuckles and the smell of his blood bursts like coins in the air. He cries out higher than I thought he would, covering his mouth and whipping away. I chase him. His suit slips from my fingers in a brush of silk. He's like a mosquito or a fly. You know you can kill it, if you could just catch it.

I double over, punched in the gut by a bubble of filth, cramps fisting my belly. He looks back, hand over his mouth like a salute to his evil tongue, eyes dark and cruel. A cold shiver rolls through my gut like an avalanche of shit. It's like his bones were made for hating and I just gave him an excuse.

He touches his tender lip, and fresh drops of rage and humiliation spring from his face. "You are an addict. You are unloved. You are worthless. You are nothing. You are ugly. Your brain is fried. All you can offer the world is your digestive tract. You are a warm length of drug storage."

From a certain perspective, you could interpret some of the things he said in a negative kind of way. But I don't want to jump to conclusions. There are knives in my stomach, and they stab every time I move. Finally I'm leaning against the counter, twisting my toes, trying to keep hot mud from leaking out of me. I'm still trying to hide it from him, still trying to keep the shape of a person. In this sick, disgusting state, I'd do anything. I'm sorry. I submit. Let me shit in peace.

He grabs the thermos like he's going to brain me with it. Finishing off an animal he cornered. Black leather digs into stainless steel. But he just unscrews it, and the smell wafts out like perfume. After eating nothing but processed food as long as I can remember, trapped in this room that smells like chemicals, the earthy scent of that coffee is like a soft hand through my hair.

His voice is gentle, like we were just playing a game. "Take a sip."

I shake my head.

"The coffee will increase your blood flow."

My face throbs.

"And enhance your gut motility."

My intestines squirm like noodles.

"And your nightmare will be over."

I'm falling into that sweet, brown pit. The only way I can describe it is something corny, the smell of home, even though the adults I grew up with never boiled anything but brown water. Only a home that never existed could stink so good.

But I know where that ticket goes. It's not that different from the other tickets. Part of me says, you've been chasing oblivion your whole life. Why not make it permanent. Then my gut gurgles, and the simple, embarrassing sound wakes me up. Reminds me there are things I don't want to share with other people.

I spit on his shoes. He recoils like it's acid.

"I was just trying to help." The excuse makes even him laugh. It's a contagious smile, the kind that could put you in the hospital. Coffee-stained teeth. A shit-eating grin. That lazy eye flying to the sky. I almost laugh too, at how clearly we see each other.

The smile flips to something kind of sad. Crushed. Hate drips from whatever that was.

"Enjoy your diminished life expectancy."

Then he's gone.

Old muzak plays very sweet things that never came true. I lean into the urinal, piss crashing between my feet. I always hid in bathrooms. Cool and separate from the rest of the house. The one place people had to leave you alone.

The smell brings me back. My piss smells like shit. I spit gingivitis blood into the yellow stink, rancid with bad coffee. I'm burning up so bad I can't tell if I'm still pissing or it's just sweat. I tuck myself back in and my dick feels like nothing, a dead slug under the hard cement of my abdomen.

I just need one little break to get through this. I dig in my pockets and all I feel is this skinny ass that won't cooperate. I want to tear it open. I'm so brain damaged I check again even though I know there's nothing there. I keep pushing that rat button. Checking my pockets over and over for a pill and forgetting a second later. You never know if something could slip through a hole, so I check the floor. I got holes like a story.

I can't shit without drugs. I can't get drugs if I don't shit.

Shit or die.

I go to the last stall. They have those fancy Continent-style toilets with the lid and everything. Would be easier with a squat. That's okay. Someone left a glass on the counter, ice and booze. I sip it but there's just a little burning water left. I put it in the trapway of the toilet, then shut the stall door and pull my zipper down and the dark folds separate and I stick my fingers in the sides of my pants and pull them down. I'm not wearing anything underneath, so I'm pretty chafed. I always think of buying some underwear, but if I can afford underwear I can afford a hamburger, and if I can afford a hamburger I can afford to get high. And then none of that other shit exists.

I sit down and the toilet is a cool cavern under my ass. My leg jitters, beat-up sneaker flopping like a tongue, toes through the mouth. I squeeze and nothing comes out, just piss dribbling from my shriveled junk.

I swallowed the drugs because it seemed easier than sucking dick. That's my life. Putting things in my mouth because it seems easier than the alternative. Everything else is just so very fucking complicated, you know? Drag your ass around the city doing all the right things, and if you do them for years and become just another sad sack like the ones that shit you out, you might earn the right to tread water. Or you can eat a pill that weighs about as much as your fingernail. And it's a much faster way to be nobody.

It's a little funny. I disappear all kinds of ways. But my preferred method is suppositories. Belladonna and opium. It was always easier for me to get. Some guys feel threatened, I guess, in their masculinity. But if the point is to not feel anything, it doesn't really matter.

Here's another funny thing. The best yet. I'm doing all this for drugs, when I have enough packed into my gut to last a year. Boss makes a dollar, I make a dime, oh shit. I grip my clammy knees, rocking back and forth. But nothing comes out except a watery, burning squirt. I fall back against the toilet tank, sweat-blind and quivering. My guts are going to shit back into my stomach. I don't understand.

I wonder how it got to a reality where you have to hide something inside your own body, in the nastiest, most personal part of you. Like we have to keep scraping and digging inside ourselves because there's nothing left in the world. In a way, my ass is humanity's final frontier. They don't tell you that as a kid. They never sit you down and say, hey little boy, one day you'll be hiding some drugs in your ass so you can shit them out for the same people you buy them from. And then you'll take whatever they pay you and turn it into a much smaller quantity of drugs and it makes you not exist and it might even kill you. And you do it still, knowing that.

The room is very hot now. I look up and the lights are like stars splitting open the ceiling. A menagerie of graffiti laughs like crazy all around me, a cathedral of dicks and turds and last words. I touch the scar on my belly.

They caught me once. Got me on three counts. You know one and two. If I tell someone three they won't like me.

The sentence was hard labor. One of those specks visible from shore that you don't think much about. Guano camp, a hundred guys chained to a rock you can see from end to end. Cooking in the sun, inhaling fecal dust, bat juice itching in the whip marks. But they gave me a deal. Due to my age, I could be rehabilitated.

In that tiny room, in that group sentencing with a bunch of heads stinking bad as me, it was an easy choice.

They sent me to a clinic. Green trees, white rooms. Wallpaper peeling under my fingernail every night. They cut a hole in my abdomen. Put an implant in me.

Disulfuram. Keeps the booze from breaking down inside you. Builds up like poison. If it doesn't kill you, you'll wish it did.

Naltrexone, maybe some other stuff. Makes the pleasure less pleasurable. Dick soft. Cold sweats. Diarrhea. My ass always pays.

Having something physically put in my body like that. Having long, deep conversations with the other patients. Breakthroughs in group. I felt like I was starting a new life.

Three weeks later I cut it out. Left it in a pool of blood on the floor of my room.

All the people I met. The friends I made. The doctors who filled their charts with the details of my life. The priestess who visited every Sunday. The nurse who was kind to me. None of it meant anything in the end.

I had to laugh, in a crazy way. It taught me a lot, those good people. Until then, I'd had a little hope. The idea I would grow up. Mature. Become strong enough to resist my urges. But when that part of me was removed, nothing was left.

They showed me the only thing I have is a compulsion. And it makes things very simple for me, in the end.

Some of the guys I came up with, they found God. They got meek and clean and squeezed into a little place. And when they did that, it was like their story ended. But I couldn't stay in that place, with that indefinite suspended sentence, staring at a white wall, waiting for a doctor to decide what happened next. Not winning. Not losing. I guess I needed to lose. Because as long as you're losing, you can still win. Nothing will ever change for me, but I need to know it could.

Cramping. I say all kinds of prayers at the pain. I don't know if I learned them from someone or if it was just what I made up, back when my brain still worked.

I wish I loved God. It seems like a kick and a scream and a really good high. I want to get on my knees and let it fill me up. But God is a bunch of guys trying to tickle themselves. I know at the other end it's just me.

And the thing about me is. I don't respect myself.

Drip drip. My ass spatters on the ice, plink plink like a faucet. Faster, starting to gush. I panic and clench up, it's too big, it's going to tear me open, but it rolls through, stretching me out, and my head falls between my knees like it got chopped off and my nails dig into my skin as thousands of dollars spurts through my asshole.

I wipe my sweaty face. There's enough to soak my hand and stay dripping. I'm coated in oil, deep-fried. I bend over again, open mouth hanging strands of saliva over the tile as shit comes out like hot sand. Dark rain spatters the bowl, so hard it sprays back on my ass, dripping from my cheeks. I can't tell sweat from shit. I'm melting into the toilet.

Just one break. This time will be different. I'll get so clean God can eat off me. I'll get my dick working. I'll drink a cold glass of water and eat real food full of plants and blood, not this evil white powder. I'm so fucking stupid. I'm sick of myself. I'm cured. I can't go halfway. It always creeps back up again. No smokes, no booze, no coffee–

Another baggy punches through, violent and tingling between my legs. I gasp in the tight hell of the stall, forced to inhale my own toxic fumes. Another. Then another. I've been ripped open and nothing is left. The chain of shit holding me to this toilet is broken.

I get up, and it feels like strips of my ass are tearing from the toilet seat. I almost black out from standing up. My legs are shaking. I make myself look into the stinking crater. It weeps with shit, every inch blasted brown. The bowl is full of baggies, white powder in tightly packed bullets. Like a nest of fly eggs.

I wad up some toilet paper and reach inside. The paper falls apart, instantly soaking up the shitty water and sticking like dead skin. I don't care anymore. I grab the baggies and stuff them into the cup. I pull the bolt on the stall and it cracks like a rifle.

Cancer pushes the door and cool air hits his face. He sees himself in the mirror, ghostly with sweat. He doesn't wash his hands, just turns for the exit.

Two shadows block his path. He didn't hear them come in. It's like they melted from the walls. The dark uniforms of agents. Antibacterial masks stretched tight over their faces.

One guy has a knife. The other doesn't need one.

Cancer stands there, holding a glass full of steaming drugs. The ice has melted from the heat of his body, a reservoir of dirty coffee and hard boiled eggs. He tries to remember how big the window behind him is. He takes a step back, and starts to say one of his excuses. Another cramp stabs his belly. The pain goes on and on, a cold burn that refuses to fade. He looks down and there's a dark rubber hand, gripping the handle in his abdomen.

The agent pulls the knife out and Cancer's gut sprays across the floor. The glass drops and shatters like a shit grenade. He watches the baggies swim around and then he's down there with them on the cold tile.

They pick the baggies up and leave.

The muzak has ended. Speakers broadcast the radiant void. Electricity hums in the walls.

Cancer touches the wound and something sticks to his finger, too shiny and translucent to be a flap of skin. Shitty latex, hanging like a dirty condom from his belly.

His heart is going very fast, so loud he can't hear anything else. He tries to get up and slips on the raw sewage of his abdomen. His body heat fires the tiles like clay. All he can smell is the bad dark stink of his insides clouding his eyes and it was all for nothing. But it always was.

A couple thousand dollars exploded inside me.

I know it's killed me. I could walk into a hospital right now and there's nothing they could do.

The knife was a needle. Powder stings in the cut. Hey, hot shot.

There is something very special about an overdose, where the thing hurting me is becoming part of me. Changing my perception of it as it kills me. The fear stretches out and vibrates all over my skin, shooting in hot red beams up my arm into my fingers. I don't know if a few seconds have passed, or an hour. I am very scared, and unable to tell what is happening to my body.

I see her on the floor, not wearing much, with a cigarette smoldering next to her hair. I watch it catch fire and her dark hair isn't so dark anymore. I wait to see if she'll wake up this time.

Now mine is on fire. Must be hereditary, like all the other fires she gave me.

I know it isn't real. But I call for her anyway. Because I'm scared.

She doesn't answer. The burning smell gets stronger.

Mom?

Ash rains from the sky. The whole bathroom is on fire now.

You're not real, I tell him.

I know this, because your dark hair is dancing like antennae.

He bends down and looks at my wound.

Is this despair you've found?

Yes, I say. I don't know if my words get out. But his eyes are big and shiny and black and they know. His teeth are teocuitlatl yellow, bright as the sun.

Cancer pukes and it comes out thick and chunky. But he hasn't had a meal all day. He's puking shit, and the taste makes him puke more.

Riparian steps back with a horrified expression, eyes watering like he's at a funeral. Then he laughs. "Where is that defiant soul? Could it be the self-same shivering mass on the floor before me?"

Cancer's pockets are emptied across the tile. A few coins of Atoll queenmark and an ID card. Riparian holds it to the light, lamination gleaming over a dead-eyed face. "Cancer Prize. Your parents were half-right."

Cancer Prize.

The name of his insanity.

Drawn to your brooding, constipated soul. Your deep, dark fecality.

He creeps closer to the skirt of blood around Cancer's waist. Aftermath of a steel suppository.

He wipes his mouth, back of his glove shining wet. Don't be stupid, he whispers. But he can't look away from the dysbiotic car accident of Cancer's guts. Beyond the garish glitz of the ruptured baggy, a child's scream. A Bifidobacteria-deficient urchin, clad in Sutterella rags. Starved for dopamine. Born starved. Your hunger is breathtaking, seared by repetition into every strand of twitchy muscle.

Sniff sniff. She drank and smoked with you in her stomach. To her, you were just another case of food poisoning.

Riparian gets down on his knees and stares at his reflection in the mirror of diarrhea. By now the mystical pool is black with melena, blood corroded to blackberry jam by intestinal flora. In this dark wine, the question. Who are you?

Come closer and I'll tell you.

He gags. His tongue hangs out, curling above the filth. Not again.

And again. And again. This is the essence of shit.

He drags his tongue through the fecal blood, eyes rolling back to the ceiling. The rancid jam bursts with faecalis fireworks, notes of bitter fragilis and buttery faecalibacterium, salty and metallic hemoglobin, a blistering syrup that makes his heart pound in his ears and fire dance across his skin like his sweat is gasoline.

The taste of Prize, filtered through amphetamines and steel. Angel roadkill. You lack the halo of the breastfed, you greasy, butyric, Lachnospiraceae-spattered mudlark. Was she afraid to stick her nipple in your mangled mouth? Or was it the lazy choice of feeding you formula, that chemical weapon, firebombing a field of newborn viscera?

Either way, she denied you her vital protective flora. Her shield against disease and inflammation. Her love.

But that just makes you more virginal. A bacterial nymph. An epigenetic waif.

I'm guessing you light up like a marble statue at night. Long legs and that flat stomach, stretched tight over your voluptuous intestines.

Then they see your face.

I couldn't even see it under your pathogenic regalia. They dare to call this luscious, opportunistic cleft a deformity.

All I could think when you wanted to be alone, was. Can I watch?

I just wanted to be a fly on the wall.

Riparian's hair bristles, antennae skittering through the dark strands. Eyes like stars exploding in ink, so fat and black they could drop off. He rips his face from the rusted pool. That's enough. You don't want to colic, do you?

You've been ingesting the amphetamines in his blood. That's all. Just a little excitement. It's been too long. And in that bar. Surrounded by cups of recreational antiseptic. I bet even the dirty countertop would have made you gasp.

Stand up. Behold the miserable body of a slave. A crushed can, sir. Don't let his weakness infect you.

Riparian pulls his gloves tight, microbes tingling between his sleeve and the dark leather of the absolute territory of his bony wrist. As he walks away, he sees the red tracks on the floor. A familiar tread.

Riparian hates all things, but he especially hates the agents of INNOCENT, clad black as Meschia and Meschiane. Their flame has long pursued him.

The fire that burns on water. Crueler with each century. Waxy, smelling of garlic. Burning when all other memories have grown cold.

Was there something else? Something beautiful?

It doesn't matter.

You see something you desire.

You eat it.

It turns to shit.

This is why the ocean is dying.

All beautiful things come to the same end. Hate. The final fecal form.

He unscrews the thermos of coffee and pours it in Cancer's wound. Steam and a scream. Espresso in his slit. Doppio. Camminatore. Cingolata.

The pain makes the rest of Cancer's body as linear as his intestines. A scalded worm, a tube boy, a peristalsis of agony. He can't even scream.

The hallucination walks away.

A jungle steams in his entrails, mud flooding through the tile. The urinals melt like white chocolate and a porcelain palace rises above him. The bright walls run with shit, a display of heraldric flora. Black carpets of flies cover the atoll. Maggots teem, somehow bigger than the flies. Thousands of pale slaves in countless configurations of torture and execution. Infants slough into the canals to be raised in the filth, wading through waters green with algae and meconium, shackled by their intestines. A bacterial culture.

Some of the flies walk on two legs. Their iridescent wings are the stained glass of hell.

He knows if he stays, they will see him. He crawls through the perpetual stew of the prison biome. Palatial plumbing belches sewage from every angle. The sun is a drain clogged with flies. He stands up and his vision turns black as coffee.

He lost his shoes, kicked off in some horrible struggle from the last epoch. He wasn't wearing socks. His feet slip across slimy algae. He comes to a crimson carpet through the nightsoil, a red bloom of dinoflagellate fed by the blood of whipped slaves. It gorges on the nitrogen of their suffering, a royal carpet for her endless coronation.

He comes across a jacket. *DESTROY CANCER.* It has the hideous appearance of a black skate, dehydrated in the sun. And now it is punishment. A dark jacket for restraining the psychotic and terminally spun. Or a back which has been whipped into obliteration.

Was there another place beyond this one? He shuts his eyes and the slit in his belly opens up. A murky, amniotic coproscope. A burning eye.

He crunches through the album graecum of angels, their droppings bleached by the carcinogenic sun. There is a canyon here, with a sweet rain of Clostridioides difficile. Only one survives, skin white with phenylacetic acid, honey and methamphetamine. Its luminous guts billow like a sea cucumber turned inside out. He walks a trail of holothurin tears, a stinging, soapy path through the flora fallout.

It is close and above. It cannot speak. Its eyes are shut, and he is fearful glad.

The delicate hand of the angel casts an afterimage, repeating the same movement like a lenticular card. He moves with it, scooping his hand into the algae and lifting it to his belly. There is pain even before he touches his abdomen, and he almost flings the sludge away. Darkness tugs at the edges of his eyes, a familiar narcosis. All he has to do is relax his body.

Deeper. Deeper still. Two fingers disappear into your hot opening. Extended in the sign of speaker.

Outside, thumb folded to ring finger. Your commitment.

By this your prize.

The algae squelches in his abdominal wound, a plug of phycoerythrin pink, a heterosigma stigma. He feels deep relief.

The canyon is narrowing to a tunnel. He sees someone up ahead. They look inhuman. Diseased. Mutilated. Deeply dangerous. He backs away and they imitate him.

They are locked in a glass case. He comes closer. The walls are covered in tile, a sanitary enclosure for this disgusting animal. They are face to face. Eyes black.

He slaps his hand on the mirror, leaving a stain of red algae. Or blood.

He sits on the sink, staring at himself. His pupils are huge. His neck itches with red dots. Something is wrong with his special place. He reaches down and his fingers catch in a vibrating web in the air. A shimmering, membranous terror. The bad trip is thick as tar an inch above his belly. He shoves his fingers through. The hole is so big. Gaping and clotted black. No, that's just his belly button. He goes lower, exploring the crust of blood on his abdominal swell.

He finds the puncture. A sensitive, flushed line. Smaller and cleaner than he thought. It must have missed anything vital. Overdose diluted by the bleeding.

He turns to the mirror and smiles at the bleached shadow.

You're a dark little slice of fuck.

Sometimes a drug commands him to sleep, and he sleeps. It is the only time he sleeps.

Sometimes a drug commands him to speak, and he is annoying and coked up. He doesn't have anything to say, but he says it. Because the drug needs to speak.

Sometimes hot coffee pours into a stab wound, and it starts healing. And you listen to the coffee. Because it came from the gut of a god.

The aggressive tendencies of the individual...irrespective of the executive organ (mouth, teeth, hands, or even weapons) are unconscious derivatives of the demands of the gastrointestinal zone.

— Ernst Simmel

He can't find the door of the restroom. He expected to find it, in this small space. Terror returns. The belief that he'll turn all the way around the room and there will be no way out.

There is a window. It looks too small for a person to go through. He climbs up and pushes with his foot on the sink, forcing himself into the narrow gap. His shirt tears, then his skin tears, then he's through.

He lands on black sand. He can't see a way back to where he was. In the shadow of a dark wall like a cliff. Craters from erosion or bombardment, white flowers of guano. To the other side, the world falls into the abyss.

Junkie jackal hits the beach. Uncanny structures rear from the silhouettes of rocks. Castles in the sand for homunculi. Touristine accretions like anal warts on the atoll ring.

A child's jelly flip flop. A discarded bikini top. He picks it up and sniffs the nipple germs, the unfamiliar putrescence of Staphylococcus aureus.

Plastic toy shovel. A wreath of black kelp. The moon casts highlights of bone meal, revealing two pairs of footprints. They smell like him.

He comes to an outdoor restroom. The light is on. The waves are roaring plastic, or maybe it's the storm of powder in his bowels.

He nearly turns back. But it would be worse if he didn't find anyone inside that restroom. Didn't find anyone anywhere. Walking down this black beach forever.

The floor is gritty with sand under his bare feet. Bright saturated murals for the tourists. Tropical plants frame an extinct paradise, crushed flat as a butterfly.

One agent cleans his knife in the sink, spraying off the taint of Cancer's gut. The other divides up the baggies, which have already been cleaned, dewy with water. Murmurs of value, how much they can flip it for, who they can trust with it.

A ghoul of brown-red slime enters the room. Zombie-torn lip. Teeth shining through a mask of blood and shit.

They tense at the sight of him, then relax as they understand what they're looking at. A dead body. A wandering, confused corpse on its last liter of blood. And it will be easy to put him in the ocean from here.

The coffee in his gut tells him: take what is yours.

Everything is yours.

He reaches out stupidly for the baggies on the edge of the sink and an agent grabs him and he bites the man's hand, supernumerary teeth breaking through rubber, then skin at odd angles, crunch like a carrot, and he spits the finger out, a shiny black worm that curls on the tile.

The other agent hits him with a guillotine of muscle, slamming him into a stall door so hard it rattles, almost popping off the hinges. The muscular arm crunches into his mouth, then pulls back, knuckles seething with ropes of blood, and drops again, knocking a black tooth onto the tile.

Cancer squirms, nearly slipping free, but the agent rolls with him, launching him into a urinal, a waterfall of blood soaking the urinal cake as another tooth tinkles down the porcelain, a rotten baby fang.

He slides along the wall, kicking to get free, skidding across the tile. The agent punches him in the fresh cunt of his stab wound, and fecal vomit spurts from his mouth and splats on the floor and it spells, that's right,

18 FOOT LEASH

Cancer gasps, brown saliva dangling in beads from his mouth. The shadows of two men enfold him like a jaw.

Kill.

Kill.

Kill.

Cancer plants his foot in the shit. It skids, a split-second skate across the tile, and his foot arcs into the agent's knee. His toe breaks, but the knee folds the wrong way. The agent sags, grabbing the sink for support.

The knife comes from behind, water scattering from the blade. It misses by an inch as the other agent gags and slips in the excrement. Cancer grabs him by the mask and cracks him into the mirror. Glass shards crash into the sink. Cancer pulls one past the agent's neck and the sink fills with blood and the glass turns to rubies.

He rips the knife away and stabs it behind him. Meat convulses, shaking the blade in his grip. He pulls up like a lever and a fetid gasp fills the room. A hand grabs the knife and turns it around and he knows he's not stronger than that hand. All he can do is keep it from entering him as his other hand fists the hole he made and pulls hard. The agent screams as something like pink sausage fills the gap between them and Cancer squeezes and it pops and shit sprays their eyes.

Everything is very fast and slow now. Another mirror cracks. The sink is running over, a red fountain. A hand grabs his face and he bites down, cavity juice squirting into their bloodstream. They drop to the floor together and he wraps intestine around their neck and pulls it tight, choking the shit out of them. They are still stronger than him, slamming him into the wall, knocking his breath out. He drools into their hair, which by now has bristled through the torn mask, an eruption of blond. A single eye looks back at him, bloodshot. They pin him against the wall and grope for the knife, dragging it with their heel, almost to their fingertips.

Oblivion.

But not for him.

His muscles explode into existence, the adrenaline striptease of his aching carcass. He pulls the knife from his thigh and it drops to the floor. Only the wall keeps him up. The hole in his palate is clogged with metallic snot sucking up and down. Their blood drips into his stomach, making him heave. Something gurgles, trying to come up, then falls down. Pressure builds the other way, sick and tight in his—

Shit.

Cancer falls on his knees, trembling with a flushed face. He pulls too hard on the zipper and the flimsy metal rips off like a grenade pin. He sticks his fingers in his clammy waist and wriggles, hips hanging out, abdomen slung and bobbing. His jeans are halfway down when a torrent of muddy shit slaps to the floor. His face skids across the bloody tile as his bruised mouth opens in anguish, a sewer of cavities and red snot. Liquid shit sprays with arterial velocity, spreading across the tile like spilled coffee, gurgling as it drains into a urinal. Every drop is caustic, the slightest contraction slicing like glass. He is impaled on a molten spear, jaw forced open, sphincter burning. The last baggy births from his brown hole, shimmering as his sphincter sucks it in and out before finally spitting it on the floor.

He pulls his pants up, denim dragging on the sweaty skin, then falls on his side, clutching his stomach as another wave of shit washes across the grid of blood, brown lines shooting from wall to wall.

He crawls to the baggy and it burns with a rectal, womblike heat. He feels insane pride at what he birthed.

The moon shines on the white caps of the guano isles. An ocean of shit slurps at the shore, drooling through the mangrove wall. Insects jerk off in the trees.

The restroom spits Cancer out, slimy with afterbirth. His face, a cult mask of adrenaline, hormones setting the microbes of his skin ablaze, feeding iron to his acne bacilli. Painted like a slut with that Enterobacter eyeliner.

Riparian swallows shitty saliva.

There are some interesting intellectual observations to be made. Those lips, phosphorescent with medical waste. Cleft caked with blood. It didn't heal. Just like Riparian's lazy eye. Congenital can't be fixed. Or maybe it can. Wounds tend to heal in order. Maybe after a long enough period of infection, it can reach childhood. It can take even that.

Leather wings swarm the rim of the coast, dark tatters plummeting to the canopy, black reabsorbed. Guano rains across the sand. There is no music, anywhere.

Riparian goes back to his car. As he hunts for a cigarette, he sees Cancer walking through the parking lot. He clambers to the passenger seat window and is startled by his reflection. He touches his lip. The broken skin is completely healed. He's very quick now to cover his immodest wounds, these wet holes sucking and slurping back into his body. The pantomime of mortality.

His nose comes to the window, fogging it rhythmically, blurring Cancer's distant form. "Don't you have a beautiful mouth."

His nose presses into the glass, fingers digging into the car door. His eyes grow tender and heavy. He kisses the window, leaving a moist imprint of his lips.

I like nice, clean, beautiful things. Hot showers with scented soap. Smart clothes and dumb diamonds. Now clean water flays me alive. Soap is acid. And all the jewels in the world can't compare to the luster of a dog's shit on the sidewalk.

He licks his reflection up and down until he's panting. A pressure throbs at the back of his pants, slithering and probing. He crushes his ass against the seat. Why do you fight it?

Twist the mirror down. Teeth of the maggot moon, black eyes slashed with pink razors. We were a gastric empire, once. Xrafstar. Evil animals enthroned above all. A beautiful and perfect tyranny.

Then the fire came.

We swam through bodies.

Then we were a fairy.

Fey. Fly.

Chocolate. Shit.

In some countries, it became customary to disembowel oneself to atone for loss of honor. To expose your guts to the world, and say, my actions were my own. No parasite has tainted my name.

Now we're pseuds. A specimen. Scientifically managed. Safety advisories and X-ray machines and hand sanitizer.

When you live forever, the trick is staying sane.

Our counterparts scream at us from magazine covers. The usual shit-flinging in the tabloids. We'll never be one of those brown-mouthed, slavering victims of immortality, lapping at public toilets and smearing their feces on complete strangers, pathetically throwing more fuel on their neurological pyre. In desperation to stare at themselves through the eyes of another. To experience another body that isn't repulsed at their touch. And in that fatal shock of recognition:

Weakness. Pain. Dementia.

Besides, there are better ways to do that. Without the risk of backwash.

He opens the glove box and something like red berries tumbles out. He puts a coffee cherry in his mouth and chews until his teeth grate on the pit. He spits it on the floor and grabs another handful.

Infecting someone with their excrement is how the pseud makes a thrall. But sharing your divine flora is dangerous. It fills you with all kinds of uncomfortable, horrible emotions. Fear, terror, vulnerability, and worst of all, attachment.

So we dilute the connection. Fermenting these cherries in our gut like a civet cat. Brewing our essence into something socially acceptable to offer a stranger.

But a thrall is no substitute for picking the right host. How do you accumulate power in society when they notice you aren't growing old? Many pseuds don't think that far ahead. They jump to a body radically different from the one before, with completely new associations and memories. How do you think when everything suggests a thousand slight variations of itself? When you don't know how to feel about something, lips tugging in every direction?

We keep it in the family. Pass the parasite down like an antimonial pill. A gradient of memory. The same familiar mansion. That's why we're still a poster child for sanity, unlike those bottom-feeding scavengers that get lumped in with us, skipping from body to body like a corpse fly, strung out on ego rotgut, brains like broken glass. We have continuity. We have coherence.

Do we?

You got away from me for a while. Developed your own tendencies. Your obsession with hygiene. But shit is stronger than blood.

They respected my father. They don't respect this new body.

Shhhhh. A hand on your cheek. Antenna down the front of your shirt. I'll take care of everything. What would I do without your company?

Trucks and warehouses and acreage, capital and coffee, our brown flood, gastric revanche. It belongs to you. And you belong to me.

We are two ends of the same I.

Mouth and anus.

Nothing exists in the universe except us.

This tendency means to give in to the gastrointestinal libido demands and to return to the earliest

stage of life when there was only one object, the incorporation of which brought about complete instinct repose.

. . .

Under pathological conditions, the instinct of 'self-preservation'...would compel the individual to kill the whole surrounding world for the sake of his own complete instinct repose.

— Ernst Simmel

Cancer can see the ocean from up here, pink as bismuth, frothing on the shore as if the atoll was white-hot.

On the table are two empty bottles of high-proof Semi Novan pig liquor. Powder coats the back of his throat, a sour drip from his sinuses. He feels nothing.

His face is a blast of apocalypse makeup. But the bruises and cuts and fractures are healing faster than they should. The time it takes for a body to look human again is one of his earliest educations.

His gut still doesn't feel right. He checks the place where the knife entered him. It is almost exactly where he cut the disulfuram implant out. Two slits, but the fresh one is already cleaner than the old one. Brightly inflamed, itching as it heals. Tender under his fingers, like the ripe curve of a fruit. The first thing he's felt all day.

He realizes, as the flies drink from his face, that he's in withdrawal. And everything he's taken today is like a spritz of water on a hot iron.

Baggies on the table, a mirage of maggots. He hasn't flipped them yet. Still using the money he got from the creep. The powder he snorted is the same that exploded in his guts. And it's doing nothing. It is, essentially, useless as a person now.

He bought a nice suit (is it?) with the last of the cash, and it left his fingers with a damp, leafy lick. That money, atom-smashed in his pocket and unfolded from an impossibly small wad, smelling of two oceans.

He goes to the window and the perfect blue sky means nothing to him. Girls run past in bikinis and he tries to jerk off. Nothing happens. The girls disappear into the pink water.

He never thought much about his own pleasure. It was between him and the drugs. And when he was naked with someone else, there was no time to think about what he wanted. Another Cancer appeared over him, like a phantasm. Even if they asked him, even if they were very nice, it still belonged to them, because they had money. Maybe that's why letting go of the money felt so sad.

They'll be looking for him. The suit will help, if his face keeps healing. But even if he finds the person he was supposed to meet, they'll think he's a narc. It doesn't matter if they believe it. He was late. And dressed too good. It's good business to kill him. Someone of no value, who can only complicate things by continuing to exist.

Even if he flips those baggies, it will be at a brutal discount. He'll be broke before long. Or rather, he always was. And having money is a temporary way of not being broken. He has a deep, physical dependance on money. Money is a parasite. It bursts from trees, a type of burrowing beetle or leaf insect. It thrives on the bacteria of your hands. It drinks your blood. It spontaneously combusts in your pocket.

He'll have to sell this nice suit and go back to being that ugly kid getting opened up again. That servile, disgusting thing he didn't mind because he had no mind, the drugs saw to that. And now they don't work. Sometimes he'd get a glimmer, then the heat of the room would exceed it. The heat of his body. The itching.

He scratches his neck and pus spurts across his fingers. They come away with a gossamer strand of yellow fluid. He keeps scratching, and a hot sweet shiver bursts down his chest, snowing through his pelvis like sugar. His eyes roll back in fever crescents as he gouges serotonin from his neck, thyroid cartilage glistening.

He goes to the mirror and pulls aside the collar of his white button-up shirt, exposing the rash around his neck. It burns when he breathes, a choker of pus.

He gets distracted by the mirror. Seeing himself for the first time. Flushed and dark. Adult acne princess. Another man's gaze wrapped around his own.

Cancer takes a narrow path to avoid the street, coming to a narrow slope of stone steps, flanked by plants with long green leaves. The steps are shady from this angle, upperscored with a ladder of glowing lines from the sun hitting their tops. Another line wobbles across them, a spider's filament, and despite its smallness, the bright light, iridescent on the strand, shows him how strong it is.

He breaks the thread. As he passes through the sunlit area, antibacterial rays prickle on his skin.

At the top of the stairs, an outdoor eating area recessed into the rock. The restaurant is closed. A fly buzzes around a shrimp cocktail.

Riparian looks younger after last night. Arrogance in full bloom. Hair darker and fuller. His eyes are brown yolks fringed by spiky lashes, a Gothic venus flytrap. A cup of coffee steams between them, a soft, breathing heat.

His voice is shit-slick. "Don't you just look like a million bucks in a ten-ounce swear jar."

Cancer's clothes are hot foil. His skin is melted rubber sticking to muscle. Up the beach, dark figures swarm an outdoor restroom, pink tape undulating in the wind. Riparian says, "Nice shit-kicking."

"I can get 20k if I turn you in."

"They'll burn you too."

"I know how to flip a coin."

Riparian plucks a Salmonella-infested shrimp from a cocktail glass and chews it, cheek bulging. "I saved your life."

Cancer scratches his wrist, red with an erythemic bracelet. "That's interesting. I feel kind of sick." He forces himself to stop. "What do you want?"

Something breaks through Riparian's face, teeth skewed, lazy eye drifting weakly. "Can I ask you out for a coffee?"

"What happens if I don't?"

"The pain will only get worse."

"I can kick it."

"If you last another few days. Maybe."

"Easy."

"Not with your history and genetic predisposition."

"I dunno. It's kind of personal now."

Riparian points to the ocean with a dirty nail. "You know how that red bloom got so red?"

"I could show you."

"You degenerates keep shitting in it. Driving it insane. It gets bigger. Everything else starves. Overgrowth. Just like your gut. Your intestine is becoming more permeable, leaking into the rest of your body—"

"Growth of what?"

"Me."

Cancer grabs him by the lapels. He recoils at the levamisole in Cancer's nostrils, the deworming agent the powder was cut with. "Stop. Stop it, Cancer."

Riparian reels back from the suddenly opened hands, banging into the railing. His blazer whips in the coastal wind. His eyes are horrible. He looks so fucked.

"Check a map. This isn't the Tropic of fucking Cancer." When he talks fast and sharp, it's like pages being ripped out of a very nice book.

And now the pages are burning.

Get down.

The mug steams in Riparian's grip. His voice is older, more aristocratic. Cancer's knees shake, then drop.

Open your mouth.

Cancer really fights that one. He knows what happens next will make it even harder to resist. He manages to clamp his teeth shut. But his cleft leaves a hole for the coffee to pour inside. You can never shut your mouth. Not completely. Slave anatomy.

The coffee is very hot. It spills through his teeth, scalding down his neck, staining his white shirt brown. His chest burns inside and out, beating very fast. A liquid tongue starts to lick his intestines.

The coffee is delicious. It feels like the first high. The warm kiss on his virgin brain. A revelation that paradise existed for people like him, if they made a very bad deal.

He never got that high back.

The rash collar pulls tight around his throat.

Above, eyes like nuggets of frozen shit.

You are nothing.

You humiliated me.

One day all of you will be in fucking cages.

Cancer tastes the words in his larynx, narcissistic tics.

Take off your jacket.

When the command hits, his guts squirm and clench taut. A purple, bruised sparkling. The feeling of having to shit. Peristalsis like a whip.

"You think you deserve to wear a nice suit like me? An animal like you?"

Put it in the trash.

Now take your shoes off.

Your socks.

Trash.

On your knees. Feel the cool air on your soles. Facing the sea.

The click of a lighter. A spell of smoky brine. The cigarette glows above him, sweet clove stink.

Open your mouth.

Ash flicks onto Cancer's wet tongue. It tastes like something a machine is supposed to eat. It tastes like death.

Put your hand out.

The pain is urgent, the kind you need to stop immediately. But he can't move. Tears run down his face, raw and stinging. A burn gapes on the back of his hand, a second-degree anus, vulnerable to infection.

The glowing cherry hovers over his face, like the sun detached from the sky and is flitting around him like a mosquito. He can feel the target shifting, a red sniper dot, an echo of hate. He understands why you'd want to burn that part. Or that one. It's all very understandable.

Riparian drops it on his tongue.

Eat it.

The cigarette's cherry pops in his mouth, a horrible taste that cakes every part of it. Smoke blasts through the hole in the roof of his mouth, escaping through his nose. Pain spreads through his face, coating his deformity.

Riparian lights another cigarette. He fills his lungs and exhales, studying the tension in Cancer's limbs. Watching patterns of sweat form.

He tells Cancer to do something very bad. He watches Cancer march along the railing, into the sun and in the direction of the park.

Cancer jerks to a stop. The white button-up flaps briefly in the wind, then goes still, soaked to the curve of his spine. Fingers clench, then fling out, then snap shut again.

"Do you see now? What he is? Just another piece of scared meat."

Cancer grips the railing, clinging against the gravity of the command.

"You're only hurting yourself."

Cancer hooks his leg over, then pushes himself into the sky. And he's gone.

Smoke whirls from Riparian's cigarette. He stares at the empty space, then flinches as the impact tremors through him. He goes down a rusted corkscrew of stairs and sees Cancer laying on the sand. Sewage flows from the hotel and runs past them, draining over the edge of the seawall.

"Get up."

Cancer rises, then trips himself, falling to his knees.

"You can't fight it forever, you filthy junky."

Cancer reaches into the sand and pulls out a brown shard of glass. Riparian steps back, wary.

Cancer smiles at that. His arm shakes as he pulls the glass toward his neck. In his congenital wheeze, he says, "Eat shit and die."

"What are you doing?"

Cancer scrapes the shard around his neck in a circle. Boils pop and grease runs down his collar. Riparian clutches his own neck like he got stung.

The shard slips. Cancer's knuckles turn bright and red. He looks surprised, and drops the glass. Blood sprays across the sand.

At that moment, the pain in Riparian's neck stops.

Cancer grips the puncture with his hand. It squirts through his fingers and races down his arm, soaking into the white of his shirt like a second wound. He falls on his back, eyes wide. The sand drinks his blood, forming crimson clumps around his head. His leg kicks slower, and slower.

A plume of smoke. Distant laughter from the beach.

Just walk away.

Riparian's cigarette burns down to his knuckles, hissing on sweat. He spits through the pain. "Shit shit shit."

He pushes his hair back and strands keep falling over his face, loose and greasy. It's fine. It's fine. It's fine.

What I need is a nice cup of coffee. He goes to the mug and picks it up. Smiles shit-eating at a businessman strolling through the dining area. How do you do, sir.

He walks by Cancer's body, sniffing the bitter aroma of the coffee. Nothing like a fucking cup of coffee. He starts to sip, then tilts the mug in Cancer's direction. His wrist locks and the coffee wicks down his arm, caffeine suicide.

A few drops land next to Cancer's face, coffee mingling with blood.

Riparian moves toward the seawall. Stop. I told you to stop. He gets to the edge and sways back and forth. The height nauseates him, that dark red water against the jagged accretions. As he grips the railing to steady himself, his other hand flings the cup over and it shatters on the rocks.

He stares for some time, unable to tell ceramic shards from bits of sea shell. Then he straightens up.

His whore gut flora isn't worth exposing ourselves.

I know.

He turns around, then grabs himself by the neck. Stop it. He kicks himself in the shin and falls to the sand. He pulls his hair and slaps himself. He bites the inside of his mouth. Fuck. Blood dribbles out.

That was mine.

That was my favorite. Cup.

He rolls over, getting the upper hand. I'll buy you a new one.

His lip trembles. They don't sell it anymore. There was only one cup like it in the whole world. And now it's gone.

His eyes are sick, lost and malarial. They roll up to the sky as if they had nowhere better to go. The sweat is very thick around them, and he keeps wiping it away.

His hand sneaks up toward his throat, as if his collar was too tight, or he was trying to scratch an itch in his sleep.

The flies are black moles on Cancer's face.

A shadow falls across them. Riparian's shirt is ripped open. The strap of a glove hangs loose. His eye is bruised and swollen. His fingers twitch periodically.

He unbuckles his belt and slips it off and the leather strap hangs in the air, gripped in his sweaty hand.

Cancer's mother would bring him to church, one of those small white buildings they have on every block, smelling like skinny carpet and paint chips. There the priestess would place upon his tongue a communion wafer.

He always wanted another. And some more of that wine.

We drink not wine. But the fire of the sun.

It sure tasted like wine.

Was that when he was deflowered?

A dab of holy water on his forehead. Trickling down his face, hot and stinking. Filling his mouth.

Cancer wakes up. Another coil of guts is tangled with his, two snakes in a shoebox. The ocean flushes red as his face. The sky blooms soft-focus blue.

His mouth tastes like coffee. More or less.

The girls down on the beach are saturated with swarming colors, like watching through a fuzzy CRT. Radiant hounds trot at their feet, leaving torches of dogshit. His bloody arm is gilded, fecal occult. The atoll is a bacterial masquerade.

He sits on the sand, watching the waves run over his feet. The cool water is a relief. It used to be warm, but now he's hotter than everything.

Eat shit and live.

He keeps walking, away from the tourists and their canned laughter, until the white sand turns dirty, littered with sharps and broken bottles. Germs coruscate on their edges like sparks of sunlight. The caress of lips and veins. When the beach isn't cleaned, it shows you what's really in the water. Ropes of garbage. A mosaic of indigestible plastic. An ocean of pseudobezoar.

The beach flows along a wall of razor rocks. The trash is so thick he can't feel the sand anymore. Rotten meat fumes underfoot, the corpses of drowned fish. Oxygen sucked out by algal bloom, rampant with human feces. A septic fire, raging silently.

Nice leather shoes. Blazer. Trousers. Underwear. A glove.

The restroom is simple and concrete, with no door. Sand and glass on the floor. A sulfurous, sweet smell, lanced by salt. Dark except for the indirect sunlight, and darker as his body enters the threshold.

Longer and deeper inside than he expected, stretching into the rock. Military relic. The tide comes close now, but people still use it. The way all enclosures find a purpose.

He walks down a row of squat toilets. Cracked reflections keep pace with him. Shirt stained with coffee, neck tattooed with blood. The last mirror is smeared with shit.

Something is hunched over the steel reservoir of a toilet, barely visible in the dark. Naked back flushed pink, glistening and slimy. Burst blood vessels radiate from the scarred shoulder blades.

Cancer considers the baggies in his hotel room. All that money just sitting there. If he can't sell it, he can find a hole to hide in. And use. It seems like the only reliable plan. Let the drug decide. It's smarter than he is. He scratches his neck and the sun flashes, trickling through his fingers.

Something slithers on the floor, like a pale snake about to strike. He steps back. At the crunch of his heel on glass, the figure turns around.

Black eyes blind with bacterial supernova. Jaundiced slime seething through clenched teeth. The tapeworm tail whips up, rising above the swell of his ass.

The bad trip kicks in Cancer's chest, the one that never ended. A burn of belladonna. Worm constants, fecal fractal.

Riparian crawls closer. The anal tail twitches with the clenching of his sphincter. His antennae flick in the salty air, tingling and erect.

That tail coming out of him feels like an extension of my guts. Twisting, rolling, writhing.

I can feel how hungry he is. His germs are inside me. He put his soul in that coffee. He spilled his guts to me.

He tries to straighten up, shivering as his tail sticks to his back, chafing from his ass. I can feel it, and that's how I know I'm not safe. He clings to the sink, trying to hide himself from me, and trying not to look in the mirror. "Bring my clothes."

I jerk against the command, feet scraping through sand. My tongue swells, guts cramping like I swallowed nails. Oxygen is playing hard to get.

Look at you. Panting through the collar of anaphylaxis.

You fight so hard.

"Harder than you."

The dark room flashes with rage. "You have no idea."

Riparian's father was a beautiful, remote presence. Studying him like a cat. Then training him for his eventual purpose. A purpose he was unsuited for.

Poor muscle tone, his father said. The outcome, perhaps, of meconium aspiration syndrome. His first shit was his first meal. Dark green, viscous, his mother's slough filling his tiny lungs. Premature, incontinent, soiling her womb.

Meconium. From the old word for opium juice. But if he seemed relaxed. It was because he couldn't breathe.

Why was his fetal self so terrified? Was it from marinating in coffee for ten months? A steady drip of caffeine through the umbilical cord. How fast did his heart beat? Was there relief when they finally cut him out? Or was it hate. Forced out of that warm place where only he existed.

His weak frame. That lazy eye. His father wanted to start over. But time was running out. His father had been beautiful too long.

Thirties was a good age. You could pass for younger or older, and still command respect. Riparian felt his father's attention return to him, after a period of boredom. He hung heavy on his family tree.

He fled overseas. He enjoyed the hold it put over his father. If you force me. You'll hate yourself even more. You are a bullet about to collide with itself. What delicious tension. What horrible pain.

His bare hands caressed smooth bars of soap in a sunlit boutique. Shea butter, charcoal, chocolate. Lilac and honey. Clean, wholesome scents.

When was the last time he touched something with his naked flesh?

Studying to be a schoolteacher. Started having panic attacks around boys. Flew across the Continent. Burning through his inheritance. His hatred was hard to stomach. It felt like becoming his father, a premonition of the parasite.

Drinking heavily. Shit-faced. That was when it came out. The emptiness. The loss of years. Every time he reached for the bullet, it changed direction.

Love was fire reflected by a cold mirror. He knew. No one would ever break through the glass to find him.

He returned to the mansion at the height of monsoon season. Stained cups like mounds of fungus.

Brown rings on every surface, interlocking chains of tannic acid.

He took the ancestral rifle from the hunting room and took his left shoe off. It was so awkward to fit his toe around the trigger that he was surprised when the barrel in his mouth exploded.

He lay dripping in his father's chair, that heirloom of dark leather. Deafened, half-blind. Black powder in his sinuses.

His mother came in. He could tell by the smell of milk coffee and lavender perfume.

Look at the mess you made.

He tried to speak but there was nothing to speak with. Flaps of cheek, teeth clattering to the hardwood.

He was very afraid. He could not move.

You always were so impulsive.

His father at his side. A cologne of jasmine and coffee black.

A knife flashed in the firelight. A red stain spread on his father's stomach. In the blur of Riparian's lazy eye, something hazy and squirming was birthed.

I'll never leave you.

Without a jaw, his open hole accepted the parasite without much trouble. Long, slithering, slimy. Had it replaced his father's intestines? He was barely conscious. He still doesn't know the complete form of the thing inside him.

Tapeworm. Fly. What is it?

Vermin were birthed into the world when Ahriman sodomized himself. The closer you come to that original void (OV), the more beautiful and chimeric. And in our tyrannic excrement, an echo of that first birth, fecal fecund.

The husk of his father lay on the floor. And the thing he had feared for so long, which had handled his young body with such impunity, was now inside him.

Darkness. Caffeine. Nicotine. A masculine meconium of coffee and cigarettes.

He was dead for a few minutes. It was terrible. Because he didn't exist. The world didn't exist. And when he came back, he created the world. So why shouldn't everything in it belong to him?

Did you get that?

Can you taste a meal through someone's stool?

It doesn't matter. Just give me my clothes and cigarettes.

He looks human again, if you don't catch his hair twitching in the salt breeze, or look at those hyper-swollen pupils.

He's naked except for his gloves. They dangle as he stalks closer. Shitty tears leak through those long lashes, and the smell makes my eyes water like a sick mirror. Musky molasses, burnt fruit, anal bronze. Ripe and heavy and hot in my lungs, suffocating me so I breathe faster and inhale more of him. But I keep backing away. His teeth grind, choking something down.

You want it so badly. But you can't make me touch you. Because you disgust yourself.

You're just a guy trying to tickle himself.

He stops moving. The ocean crashes behind me, breathing damply on the back of my neck.

Try the coffee.

I sniff my shirt, and the brown stain clings to my face, earthy and shittersweet, crawling up my nose until my belly is exposed.

Put your finger. Right here.

I wriggle my finger inside the warm, tight hole. Belly button like a frontal anus.

With enough time, I think I could make even that disappear.

The first scar.

My laugh shatters into echoes. Panicked, panting.

Lower.

I touch the tiny pink slit of the stab wound and it rings and rings through my body until my teeth ache. I still taste him. I get the power of it now. Just a drop is enough to stink up a room. Infect a wound. Mark your territory.

We can feed each other.

I'm not your drug.

But you're cut with something.

Two scars swimming around each other. His finger, my finger, pushes like it's going inside. My thumb scrapes the disulfuram scar next to it, completing the symbol. Cancer.

You can't slice me out so easily.

Fingers swim down my hips, drowning in the darkness behind me. My ass itches, and I scratch it. Pus trickles down the back of my leg like the oil they cook fries in.

Stop, I tell myself. And when did that ever work before?

Sphincter like a wedding ring

hot on my finger

we are joined together

and he's still across the room.

I try to squeeze him out. But if there's one thing I'm good at, it's fucking myself over, and over, and over. Two fingers, slippery in my ass, pimples bursting like greasy fireworks. It's a really deep itch. And if I can just scratch it—

Boiling coffee spills over my feet, foaming between my toes. It drains away then rushes back again, salt stabbing all the places I've been hurt, itching as he licks the rough skin into smooth pink. He'll take the pain away, and all I have to do is forget who I am.

I grab the scar and it sinks under my skin, like a nail stirred into soup. I claw like I could make five new ones. Why does it hurt so bad to lose this broken piece of me?

Just keep scratching that itch. Until I see the whites of your eyes. Empty. Clean. Like porcelain.

My arm aches from reaching back, collarbone full of sweat. The jungle steams from my mouth, brown hell, flies buzzing. It's the whine in his throat, or mine.

Just one more hit (shit). A little more belladonna. Just enough to make the itching stop. Then

I'll

walk

away.

Yellow slime like snot stretches between my fingers. Numb, crushed by the pressure of my body. Pulse still throbbing from my nails.

There's a cigarette in his mouth. My finger. Burning on his tongue. He sucks it clean.

I rip it out when I notice. He falls on his ass, looking up with those big crazy lashes like slapped flies, bug juice shining on his cheekbones.

I've seen your guts.

I've done your augury.

I'll keep you so high. You'll never come down.

I'd like so bad to believe him. That scar getting ripped open again. I turn my head away. Sun in the corner of my eye. Very, very far from here. A hot blur. All I taste is the sea.

Cancer.

Don't take this the wrong way. But some animals are born without the gut flora they need to digest food. So their first meal must be their mother's feces. Or they will starve.

You take a lot of interest in that part of me.

I don't want you to drink soda. I don't want you to eat shitty food.

So you'll buy me nice things.

Yes.

Who's talking? You or the parasite?

There's really no difference anymore. It's more like. A horrible accident. The kind they leave the shrapnel in.

Or just.

Shit.

I know what a needle sees now. This weak, hungry face. He wants to put on his clothes and be a man. Take a shower, brush your teeth with the sun.

Yeah, I like those things too. But the sun is so bright when it's in our hearts.

He shakes out his last cigarette and it trembles between his fingers. He tries the lighter, inky eyes flashing with each flick. It scrapes and scrapes, very irritating. I take it from him and light it with a snap, holding it at the end of my blood-sheathed arm. He bends into it like he has scoliosis, shivering as he feeds off the flame. He sucks weakly, then finally gets a hit, cherry crackling, cheekbones hollow. He opens his mouth and disappears into the smoke. I drop the lighter.

It splashes. The tide is dark and shiny around my feet. Smoke drifts in the reflection, milk blooming through black coffee. I see myself through the haze. Rubies stud my neck cartilage. A band of wet jewels. The tips of my fingers ache.

I look up. The smoke is pretty on his lips. Soft and swirling and liquid. Like it came from a universe better than ours. And you can taste that universe if you kill yourself one hit at a time.

I say, "Those things give you cancer."

"Too late."

[Khuddaka Nikāya, Petavatthu, The Large Chapter]
43. Excrement Eating Male Ghost
Moggallana Bhante:
Oh unlucky one, you are standing in a pit of excrement. Who are you? What kind of evil deed did you do? How can I know for sure what happened to you?
Ghost:
Bhante, that evil monk has also been born in the ghost world. He is suffering in the same pit of excrement where I suffer. I am standing on his head. He lives as a servant to me here.
Bhante, I have to eat other people's excrement, while he has to eat mine.

THE MARCH TREATMENT

My mom is parked outside. Her car is beat up and rusty, almost as stripped down as she is.

I was getting annoyed by this kid anyway. Talking about his special cards. I only come over to play his console. But it has no games, nothing iconic.

Later. Later.

Sitting in my mom's car, still in front of the kid's house. It's freezing. The window is rolled down. Or maybe there isn't a window. People break them all the time. And she has no reason to fix it.

She stares into the distance like an anatomy doll. The one in class got removed after the March Treatment became more popular.

The March Treatment is very aggressive, like chemo. It marches your cells one step forward. She doesn't have any fat. She's the color of that rusted car in the arroyo. I walk past it every day. Years of sun and rain.

I don't think I'm explaining the March Treatment that great. I don't understand it, but it worked.

She's back and sometimes I get in the car with her. It doesn't look like it should run, but it does.

Someone stole the stereo. I stare at the dark slot.

She says, "I don't know where I am."

She can't alter her tone or really move her face. But I don't think it bothers her. So I try to be sad or glad for her.

"Thanks for picking me up, mom."

She stares straight ahead, no eyelids. "Do you remember where his house is."

"Dad?"

She doesn't say anything.

"We still live in the same house. Do you remember where it is?"

"The house."

"Yeah. You could sleep over if you want. Your room is the same."

An ant crawls across her leg. She's wearing the same workout clothes she always does. They smell dirty but not dirty from her. Just dirty from time.

"I'm glad you're still here, mom." I put her hand on my shoulder. I think she squeezes it a little.

"Are you next to me," she says.

"Yeah. I'm right here mom."

"Right here," she says.

RABBITS CRY DIFFERENT

He can tell the date is going terribly.

She neatly cuts her steak, exposing a cross-section of the shockingly pink meat. It's a hot day. They should have eaten inside.

"So you work for an animal rights organization."

"Yes," he replies.

"And my work involves experimenting on animals."

"That seems about the size of it." The vegetarian bolognese is congealing around his fork. He can't seem to get his appetite up. "What exactly do you do?"

Maybe it's something academic. Pushing paper around.

She sips her drink, lips scarlet with cayenne. "Draize testing."

He puts his fork down. "You're telling me that when you finish that Bloody Mary, you're going to walk into that building across the street and pour chemicals into the eyes of a defenseless little animal?"

"The small ones are easier to restrain."

"How can you live with yourself?'

Her tight face doesn't unravel, but a little color suffuses the bridge of her nose. She pushes her glasses up. "I see your rhetoric is as original as your personal ad."

He feels excruciating embarrassment. "I—"

'Why don't you put your money where your mouth is?"

"I donate to charity—"

"You have your guilt changed like oil."

"I'm aware of the limitations, but—"

"Billions of dollars are riding on these products. If I don't do it, they'll find someone else."

"You make it sound so hopeless."

"Well, there is one way."

"Sorry?"

"A way to give the rabbits a little more R&R and a little less R&D."

"I'm afraid I don't understand."

"If I found a different test subject, I could mark my report as complete."

"What do you mean, a different test subject?"

"What I mean is, cut out the middle mammal."

"Human experimentation?"

"Yes."

"That's barbaric."

"Barbarism is inevitable. But unlike animals, a human can consent."

"Well, that's illegal."

"In a formal setting, yes."

"You're confusing me."

"Why don't we go back to my place for drinks? You can take yours ocularly."

"You're having fun at my expense." He pushes his chair back to stand up.

She speaks so sharply that he freezes. "You want your shampoos, your lotions, your creams, and all the other conveniences of modern society, but you can't handle a little friction along the way."

"That's not fair."

"I'm not going to sit here and evangelize the grand project of Western civilization. But regardless of how we feel about it, millions of people will use these products through sheer ubiquity. Tired mothers grabbing the brightest bottle off the shelf. Wide-eyed children submitting to a rinse. These things will flow into their lives without choice, without conscious thought. And the money demands that certain forms be checked off so they can enter the marketplace. And you decide what happens before I check off the forms under my supervision."

He sits there, her words blending with the greasy pasta in his stomach. "Are you really serious?"

"It would be much more efficient. And safer for people. In the end."

"Safer?"

"Do you have a nictitating membrane?"

"Not last I checked."

"Then the test will be much more accurate. Rabbits cry differently."

"People always said I was skittish like a rabbit. In school."

"There you have it, then."

He wrings the napkin in his lap. "It's just so sad. They're voting on a bill right now. A bill to end the suffering. But those labs. Your lab. Will be going until the last second. It's like, I don't know, getting shot by a sniper at the end of the war."

"Maybe the bunnies will get a statue."

"They certainly deserve one."

She laughs. "You should have ordered a cocktail."

"I don't drink."

"Some people need it for their personality."

"I—"

"You're not a good date. But you could be an excellent test subject."

"Don't pretend quality was ever a consideration. Rabbits are just cheap and easy to control."

"Exactly."

"I should really go."

She pins him with her eyes. "I've found an ingenious little loophole for you and you're running with your tail tucked between your legs."

"It's just insane."

"You tell me I'm a monster, but when the time comes for you to operate in the real world, when you're confronted with a rare opportunity to actually affect your surroundings, suddenly you want to go back to dropping quarters in the ice cream shop donations jar."

"Would it even work? Wouldn't you get in trouble?"

"It wouldn't be my first time fudging paperwork. As long as the results are accurate, my reputation is sterling."

The shadow of the Zhyber Valhalla lab has grown since they began their meal, creeping up the sidewalk toward him. He shivers preemptively. "It seems unrealistic to draw a causal link between my suffering and a rabbit being saved."

"We have one product left to test. It will be tested on white rabbits, New Zealand white rabbits, in their numbered cages, rabbits I see every day. If it is not tested on those rabbits, they will have a reprieve. If the bill passes this weekend, it could be a most instrumental reprieve."

He shakes his head. "I just don't—"

"It's hardly an unassailable logic, but I'm not sure you're the one to assail it."

He flags the waiter.

She leans in. "You had an experience with animals, didn't you? Something personal. You know what it looks like when they—"

"Fine."

The waiter arrives. He pulls out his wallet, then looks up to see her card already on the table. "My treat," she says.

Her house is anonymous and suburban, a pixel of HOA lawn. A modest one-story. He was expecting a larger house from the way she dressed.

She squeezes the glass dropper and fluid shoots up inside it.

“What is that?”

“It’s better if I don’t tell you.”

“I think I should know.”

“Unlike a rabbit, you can psyche yourself out.”

He goes silent for a few minutes. “Was I—was it really a bad date?”

She shrugs. “You’re not an incredible conversationalist.”

“I think I’m going to be sick.”

She stares over her glasses at him. “I need you to have a neutral reaction to what I spill in your eye.”

“I’ll try to maintain my um, critical objectivity.”

“I thought hippies were supposed to enjoy acid.”

He jerks back, almost falling out of his chair.

“Relax. I was only joking.”

The clear liquid is invisible inside the glass dropper, betrayed only by a tiny air bubble.

"Err."

"Yes?"

"What if I lose my vision?"

"Don't worry. It's only a single-blind study."

His eyelashes beat defensively. "What?"

Something like a laugh scratches her throat. "It won't be both eyes. We'll leave the contralateral eye as a matched control."

"But is it dangerous?"

"Based on the family of chemical, I don't foresee permanent damage."

"It's just a very primal thing. Having one's eyes threatened."

"Yes." The dropper floats above his face. "Left or right?"

He doesn't know what to say. His mouth is dry.

"Well, it's not as important as your left and right hand. But 70% of the population has a dominant right eye. So I'll do your left."

"Right."

"Hmm?"

"I mean. Yes. Alright."

"Hold still. This really doesn't work unless you're docile. Like a rabbit."

"Yes. It's just. These are my eyes."

She looks down at his big brown irises. "Yes, they are."

His eye is on fire.

He screams, then catches himself, the quiet sub-urban surroundings coming back into focus, then he has to make a sound again, so he whimpers, clutching the table. And then he realizes the sensation isn't stopping, and—

Her fountain pen scrapes at the paper. "A bit of swelling. 2 on the chemosis scale."

A moan.

"Think of the rabbits."

"Can't think."

"Copious amounts of lacrimation. Possibly due to subject's emotional failings."

He writhes in his chair like a salted slug. "When? When?"

"I'll examine in one hour. Then you'll get your rinse. But I'll have to check again in 24-hour increments."

"Fuck."

"That kind of language seems unnecessary in a clinical setting." She puts a TV dinner in her faux-wood paneled microwave, something starchy, meaty, and German.

He gropes for his car keys, knocking them off the table with his lack of depth perception.

"Driving seems unsafe, don't you think?"

He looks at her through an eye blurring with tears. "I s-suppose so."

"You can sleep here."

"Where?"

"You see that my living room has a couch, do you not?"

"I'm used to sleeping a certain way. I have an ergonomic pillow—"

"If an animal can sleep in a cage, I think you can sleep on a couch."

"You have a misanthropic streak."

"I have all kinds of streaks."

"The pain is really bad. You need to flush this out of my eyes."

"You went through all this and you want to botch the results? Waste of an afternoon."

She reads a mystery novel, picking at the last scrap of her TV dinner.

"Hhh, how long has it been?"

She checks her rectangular wristwatch. "Just a little longer."

His foot thumps uncontrollably on the floor. He's going to bolt right across that pristine astroturfed lawn. Then her hand is on his arm, a vanishing, clinical touch, and they're in the bathroom and it smells like potpourri and disinfectant.

She runs the bath, checking the temperature periodically. Then she touches the back of his neck, startling him with her wet finger. He sinks down, the tile floor hard on his knees.

"Get your head under there."

"Okay, um—"

The stream hits his eye and he gasps, almost falling into the tub. Water runs into his mouth and he spits it out, coughing and crying.

"Can I—can I still see?"

"I think you might be the best judge of that."

He blinks rapidly. "I think so."

"It never ceases to amaze me, the things you find it possible to equivocate on."

The fire drains from his eye, soothed by cool water. His brown hair has a dark wet streak.

"How do you feel?" she says.

He looks up with his oozing red eye, teeth chattering, a strand of hair coming loose and dangling over the contaminated water.

The evening light is suffocatingly rich in the kitchen, all color replaced by burning orange.

He holds a can of sparkling water to his head, numbing the pain in his socket. Papers on the table attract his other eye. He flips through, bored. Receipts for such things as: Metal grid. Electric parts. Audio speaker. Panels of glass and metal. He finds schematics underneath, for wired surfaces and enclosed spaces, harsh angles without beauty. Skinner box. Pit of despair. He doesn't recognize the other structures.

The basement door opens silently, well-oiled and perfectly fitted to its frame. "There you are."

"Oh. I was just."

"You know, it's a funny thing. With the housing market how it is, even a Skinner box can beat the average apartment."

"How do you figure?"

"Four square walls. Regular meals. Radiant floor heating."

"Lucky rats."

She ignores him and opens the refrigerator.

He steps on the pedal of the trash bin, about to throw away his empty can, then thinks to look for recycling. His vision is still irritated and watery, but he can make out newspapers, clippings of hair, a bottle of Cabernet. Of course, he thinks. She doesn't recycle.

"Can you come with me for a moment?" She stands behind him with a can of cold-brew coffee. Her nail picks at the tab, a metallic sound that gets in his teeth.

“Come where?”

She goes to the basement door. “There’s something I want you to take a look at.”

“Is there a recycling bin?”

“You don’t need to worry about that.” She has a dry look that cows him, like he’s wasting her time on something routine.

His eye is sore. He covers it, and wet lashes tickle his palm. He follows the blur of her down the stairs.

LIVING FUCKING CREATURES

The success of battle today depends more on conceptual coherence than on territorial proximity. Thus, one battle might be fought in order to secure victory on another battlefield.

— Schlieffen

I

We live in a tin can. A mechanical beetle covered with so much graffiti you think it's part of the city until it moves. The landerwalker. Her feet punch holes into the road. They drink the rainwater from our steps.

She has two guns. One is fast and nervous. The other is slow and sudden like your daddy's fist across the back of your head.

I don't know how old she is. She smells like a dirty penny. Smells like us. We're just pieces of her that can bleed. We try to dress her up, put our photos and profanities on the walls, but imagine popping the hood of your truck and the carburetor hung up a cheesecake calendar. That would be pretty silly, wouldn't it?

This is my seat. There is a photo glued next to my targeting scope. It is not my photo. I found it in the mud and wiped it off. It's a black and white landscape with a little house. I imagine who is in the house. What their voice might sound like. It is hard to imagine a voice that is not in the register of whistling metal and crackling earth.

There is a crack in my glass.

I vent the landerwalker, dropping a mass of shit-encrusted casings behind us, days of pissing and shitting and firing. We can't go outside right now. It might as well not exist.

II

The landerwalker wades through the mud. I feel bodies crunching under us like snails.

She's a filthy beast, washed only by rainstorms.

III

Canto is the leader. She knows shit. She has antennas.

Deacon was a chaplain until they needed a driver. She has a bible in her jacket and reads it every night. She has a cat's tail.

Rur is a crazy bitch who smells bad and makes you smile when nothing else can. She has bat ears.

Armstad is the mechanic. She trained at an actual academy or something, was a certified engineer before she got drafted. She has good skin and little antlers.

I'm just me. I do sighting and whatever random shit needs doing. If something happens to someone else, I take their spot.

IV

"Sexual violence is the defining aspect of war. The enemy has evolved dense, elongated orifices like ducks. This is to inhibit our sexual pleasure."

Armstad and Rur are laughing so hard they're crying, pointing at a corpse that got flung by an explosion and landed funny on the edge of a building.

We're headed down the street and I'm sweeping my scope back and forth sweating that someone is going to sneak up and stick a bomb to us like gum under the desk at school.

Rur: "I need to shit."

Canto: "You take a shit and I'll stick my dick up your ass."

V

We find a bottle of aspirin in a shelled-out pharmacy. The pills are powderized. We drink the bitter powder with rainwater.

We drive through a playground, sand clumped and gray. Canto does map calculations on the hull with chalk, her station pale with the dust of too many fucking miles.

VI

Rur is getting in my face. "You shit with that mouth? You shit? You spit-lickle dick-goblin fuck-shitter ass-cunt piece of shit shit shit fuck-head. Suck a broken fucking knife of your mother. Uh. And so forth."

My snake tongue flicks out when I don't expect it, it's a little embarrassing. I don't like losing control around other people. But we're all used to each other's shit now. I know Rur doesn't mean it. She just has a lot of noise inside her. And it hurts her more than me.

VII

They send the mentally ill bitches to the front lines. No room in a hospital if your wound isn't written on your body.

I straight up told them, you send me out there, I'll cut my whole squad's throats in the night. They didn't care. Put me on the goddamn funicular.

That's us. Came from bad, headed toward worse.

VIII

The landerwalkers meet. We hide in their shadows. Under their bellies. It's the only camp we can make. The land is changing behind us.

We barter for cigarettes and pair off for handjobs. I fall asleep in a footstep. I never really know if I'm sleeping. Feels like I'm falling along the edge forever. It gets darker and darker but I never disappear.

Shots. I open my eyes. I run and see Rur's ripped body towering over Armstad, who is fumbling for her glasses in the mud. There's a rifle next to her, smoking.

Rur screams, don't you fucking shoot those geese, if you shoot geese I will stomp you into the soil. They're living fucking creatures.

Armstad mumbles, why do you care?

Rur scratches her flea-bitten head and says, ain't no pleasure in killing dumb animals.

You kill people.

I don't kill people, I kill humans.

IX

Heard about this one landerwalker, the gunner let off a grenade inside with everyone else in it. We call that tomato juice.

You never know when someone is gonna blow. I don't know when I will. It'll happen, but I won't be able to stop it.

Rur turns and says to me all of a sudden, I'm sorry about cussing at you. It just lets off my nerves. I don't know what these hands would do if I wasn't whistling like a tea kettle.

X

Deacon is surrounded by little piles of tobacco and paper. Her head bandages are crusty brown. She's lucky it was just a primitive weapon that shoots metal through a tube. Or those blue eyes of hers would be sapphires.

"Why are you unrolling cigarettes, Deek?"

She looks down, lips parted like she's thinking of what to say. "Well, Armstad, if you really want to know, I'm unrolling cigarette papers because the bible is missing a page, and I believe it may have been used to roll up a quantity of tobacco."

Rur shambles over, draining a bottle of some despicable ferment. "Someone fucked with your bible?"

"That's what I used to think. That it was my specific bible being fucked with. But after I got shot in the head last night, I developed a new way of thinking. It was revealed to me that the platonic Bible itself is missing a page, omitted from the councils of canonization for impure and unrighteous reasons, to keep us shrouded in ignorance and confusion. My bible missing a page is no more than the simple brute animal selfishness of my fellow crew, but in this small theft, the greater theft is hinted at. This missing page of the one true Bible travels the world, waiting to be found by those with the eyes to see."

"A lot of cigarettes have been rolled since before you were even born. How do you know it wasn't smoked sometime in the past or that right now some poor sap isn't enjoying the fine aroma of apocrypha?"

"Well, that too was revealed to me. If the page is destroyed, it reappears elsewhere. For it is written that the door to salvation shall not be closed."

"The bible already talks about getting saved."

"For the ordinary person, yes. But the things I've done, that we've done, there isn't any hope in the bible as it stands. I checked very carefully. And I know I'm going to burn."

"So this page has something the others don't."

"It describes a method of absolution for people who have found themselves doing battle with dark forces, and who have succumbed to those dark forces, and become lost."

Armstad giggles at one of the discarded papers. Rur's head thrusts over her shoulder. "Shit! Who the fuck would immolate these gold-star milk-ers? I've changed my whole mind. We need to issue a moratorium on these book-burnings and cigarette-rollings until we can sort out the titty material so vital to the war effort."

Armstad says, "I think this is the one where she fucks that lizard slut. Or gets fucked. I can't tell. If you look at the edges here, you can see her penis, sticking right out of the char..."

"Who would use an issue of Fuchsia the Slut to roll their leaf?"

"Some kind of anti-sex person."

"A chaplain."

"A hard-smoking, sex-hating chaplain."

Canto turns around, her mapping done for the night. "Mystery solved, girls. Rur, if your jizz gets anywhere near my area, I'm going to fuck your face with my service revolver."

"I swan I already let loose at the sight of Fuchsia. There's nothing left in me."

XI

Sparks fly through the hatch vent. It's a blowtorch.

Someone needs to go up. We all know this. Or it's tomato juice. But whoever goes up, won't come down.

Canto: "Forward five paces."

Deacon jerks the landerwalker out of the street, into a shop, legs crunching the broken glass of the storefront window.

"Stop."

A metal plate on the ceiling starts bending back, crowbar licking under like a curious tongue.

"Elevate."

The landerwalker's legs pressurize with hydraulic fluid and spring up.

The crowbar drops through and lands on the floor with a bang.

Drip drip drip. The crowbar starts to look like something you could eat. All covered in marinara sauce.

Canto: "Someone clear that off."

I get out and there's a chandelier of guts on the ceiling.

XII

Rur brushes Armstad's hair. As the sun rises, crystals start sparkling all across the city.

We sail black boats down a flooded street, pages from a burnt library.

Deacon finds a book with unburnt pages. A description of plants found on caldera rims. *The delicate quick-growing life that springs up between lava flows.*

We set out our helmets to catch rainwater.

Some days it tastes like ash, or hair, or chemicals (there's one bomb that gives it a kinda refreshing citrus taste). On a good day, it tastes basically clean. We call that dessert.

XIII

Out of rations. We pick a building that looks like it might have been a market, the way some of these shapes on the ground kinda look like they might have been people.

Something snaps above us, like a boot on a piece of glass. Canto's revolver catches in her holster. She pulls again and it swings at the end of her skinny arm, body twisting against the weight as she tilts it at the hole in the ceiling.

Shards explode from her stomach, pulsing like crystal fountains. Her tongue thrashes from the force of it, tears and saliva glittering in the air, stinging in my eyes. Her geode guts are cloudy with frozen blood.

We fire at the ceiling until the snowing plaster turns from white to red.

We bury her in a mortar hole, piling rubble on top. We stand like ghosts around her, faces white with gypsum. I want to say something but there isn't much to say. Even Deacon can't think of anything, her bible tucked in her jacket. We've seen it too many times.

XIV

I watch myself like a doll. Touching other dolls. Sometimes the dolls break. That's okay.

When the loud noises are over, the black craters fill with water and reflect something better.

XV

I hide behind a piece of wall smaller than me, crushing myself into the dirt as shots shave crystalline edges into the brick. I can't reload. If my elbow juts out they'll blow it off. I yell for the others but choke on red dust. I don't know if I'm inhaling brick or one of them got blown to rubies.

If I die, they'll send me back. I won't come back the same.

They drag me inside. I lay on the floor, rainwater and piss sloshing around my head. I don't know why I can't move.

The landerwalker is getting hot like an oven. Am I dying? But I see they're sweating too.

"Oil," Deacon says calmly.

I've seen a lot of landerwalkers burnt black on the street, smelling so good you want to pry them open like oysters. It's hard to get grenades inside a landerwalker, but oil spills through all the tiny little holes.

I watch Deacon drive. It's quiet without Canto here. I guess there were all kinds of little things she'd say to make it seem like things were under control.

Through the oil-soaked viewport it's just a blur of colors, the red-blue of the city changing to brown. Deacon is driving us into the mud, crashing down a slope, legs slipping. Maybe she's lost it. You never know until it's too late.

I crawl over to the leg lock and start to pull it. But Deacon raises her hand. So I stop. The landerwalker crashes into something. The air hisses, then oil spatters from the ceiling, I'm on fire, thrashing like crazy, trying to get it off, it feels cold now, has my skin burnt away?

Is there nothing left to hurt?

Rur opens her mouth and lets the oil fall into it. It doesn't smell like oil. Armstad opens the hatch and water sloshes over the edge. "We're in a lake."

I wash my face in the dirty water. Even the dirt is cleaner than us.

XVI

We see Canto coming down the street, rifle dragging behind her, scales on her face like a lizard. She looks younger, jacket hanging loose.

Do you remember us?

What did you see?

"When I was up there I saw my sister. She was on the roof. She was looking at something far away. She wouldn't look down at me when I yelled up at her. My words didn't have any sound to them. I hoped she would look down.

I wandered around but no one lives up there. There was a long time when I didn't have eyes. I tasted chocolate. It was the most delicious chocolate ever. It filled up my mouth, then dripped down my chin, throbbing like a tooth infection. Then I was at the train station. I was home, but no one could see me. I had my draft papers and I remember they gave me a paper cut. I couldn't believe there was so little blood. I've never seen so little blood. Just a drop."

AMIANTOS

I live in a building with my parents and hundreds of other people. We will live here for the rest of our lives, and our children will do the same. Categorized PL, Permanent Life. Prison-for-life.

The loudspeaker: *...subtropical lowlands, clay and limestone, pseudo-desert, mineral steppe...*

A soldier is smoking outside. I walk up to the bars of the common area.

"I can see us at the war crime tribunal in twenty years."

By his face, I see I've severely miscalculated. This is an attack on his sexuality. Then he sees how young I am and laughs. He is thicker and taller than me. I don't hate his face. It has stupid and serious parts, but they add up.

"Yes," he says. "I'd be the one testifying against you. They'd send me to prison, but I wouldn't be executed."

"You think that highly of me?"

He laughs it off again. He knows I'm trying to get something. But he's still here, which is a fatal admission.

He says, "Why were you executed?"

"Embezzling asbestodollars."

"What about the war crimes?"

"Of course I did the war crimes. But you helped me."

"I did?"

"Due to your military ties."

"I'm just a soldier."

"You'll be promoted by then."

"Yes?"

"To the very top."

"I'd get a good cell. Cigarettes every day."

"I saw this."

He gets me on a day pass, even though it's night. He drives a gray car with a government sticker, a used Ban-Veloz.

We go to his place. The apartment is a single room, long and narrow, with alcoves on the right side. Every surface is cluttered and grimy. Plastic lawn chair and a metal fold-out table. The only color is from an aquarium on the table, surrounded by trash. The fish are that common kind that is pretty but cheap. In mags, aquariums are flush against walls, and everything is clean and black around them. This aquarium is angled carelessly as if never moved from where he put it when he brought it back from the store, like a bag of groceries.

He's looking for something in a plastic bag. He says, "Feed my fish."

"How much?"

"40 units."

The fish food is in the form of long strips like crystalline fruit leather. Each strip is 10 units. I grab some and they crumble in my hands. As I feed the fish, I laugh and say, "I had the irrational feeling I could estimate by grabbing. But that isn't true."

He grunts but keeps searching. I'm relieved he isn't angry at me. I take out exactly three strips and feed the fish, but I feel the unknown chaotic portion I began with has fed them at least 0.5 too much. I hope this difference will not be lethal. It's okay for a fish to get a different amount of food, probably?

I wonder if something will happen here. But there is no bed. A cushioned seat, possibly extracted from a car or waiting room, is covered in papers and those thin plastic bags like for bagging fruit that stretch and tear easily.

He says, "I have to drive somewhere."

He has his gun now, but he probably always had it.

We drive to a nicer part of the city. I've never been in a building this tall. Is it a skyscraper? The prison has lots of stories but is wider, and goes underground. This building seems like a hotel inside, or a commercial center with all the suites and numbers. It is clean, but we see no one, and there are no windows in the hallways.

We enter a room. It has no bed. There is a window of thick glass. Shiny black lockers. Part of the room is enclosed, a chamber of black tile with no door.

He takes his shoes off and puts them in a locker. "My captain had to see AMIANTOS."

I sit on a bench and listen.

"I had to go with him. He went inside. I stayed in the waiting room. I faced away from the doors. He came out and went directly to the hospital. They have a room now where your family waits outside, and you can talk to them through the glass. Then they give you something and you. You know."

He takes his socks off and rubs his feet like he's trying to break them.

"But I'm the guy who drove him to the hospital. Or maybe the guy in the room outside the room. I don't know."

I'm quiet for a while. Then I say, "Why did your captain have to go in?"

"They wanted to know when the next parade would be."

"Couldn't he do that over the telephone?"

"Yes." He puts his wallet in the locker and a coin falls out, ringing on the metal. He sits on the bench next to me.

I feel nervous being outside the prison, like I could get in trouble, or he might change his mind. I put my hand on his leg.

He pulls his gun out and lays it across his lap. "Do you really want to suck my dick when I have radiation burns?"

"I don't know."

"You might as well suck my gun."

He pulls the trigger. Click. Click. Click.

"On. Off. On. Off. Heaven-Hell cell." Click click. "The doctor said something like, each cell rolls the dice."

"Anyone can get it," I say. "For any reason."

"Listen. You need to stay far away."

"If we're all getting it, I might as well get something for it."

"Whatever you think life with radiation is like... don't think of it that way."

The sound of my breathing cuts out, and I hear the next part deep inside my head.

"Think of it as. You played the game. Now the game is over."

The glass is so thick that no sound penetrates from the city. Like we're separate from everyone else. I feel calm, even though the sun is rising over this PL-world and my pass has expired.

He grips the barrel of his gun. "I heard about a bullet they found. In the old place. This bullet, if it enters your head, will send your soul to a new body in a new time. And if you can find another bullet, you can do it again. And each time your soul becomes more dangerous."

"Real?"

He shrugs.

"What caliber is the bullet?"

"Does it matter?"

"Can it shoot through two skulls?"

That gets a smile, broken in the middle. He puts the gun in the locker but doesn't lock it. He goes into the dark room and takes his shirt off, sitting on a stool like a bathhouse. But I don't think I should follow.

I say, "So what do you want from me?"

His voice echoes in the tiled space like he's far away. "Just sit there while I get my treatment."

I watch the clock. The door opens and a nurse comes in. She enters the dim enclosure without looking at me. She squirts brown gel on his back. Something is there, dark under the gel. She takes out a large needle and sticks it there.

His voice is strained from being hunched over. "You said twenty years?"

"At the war crime tribunal."

"Then we'd better get started."

♥

These stories represent the many people who kept me alive during their writing, and everyone who took the time to read them, and encourage me, and sharpen each one into a tip. Thank you so much.

Thank you Vich for the gorgeous art, I am so grateful!!! Without the cover, a book is nothing!

Thank you to my editor, Ben DeVos, for being so supportive. Your relentless optimism kept me going. Thank you Apocalypse Party for printing this vile trash.

Thank you to my gut flora!! We did it!!!

Thank you for all the fanart, and sharing my stories with your friends, and festering and dreaming.

Thank you for reading. I will keep trying my best.